NANCY DREW
AND THE CLUE CREW®

"MY CLUE CREW AND I ARE WILLING TO DO WHATEVER
it TAKES TO BRING THAT EVILDOER TO JUSTICE."
- NANCY DREW

PAPERCUTZ™

NANCY DREW GRAPHIC NOVELS AVAILABLE FROM PAPERCUTZ

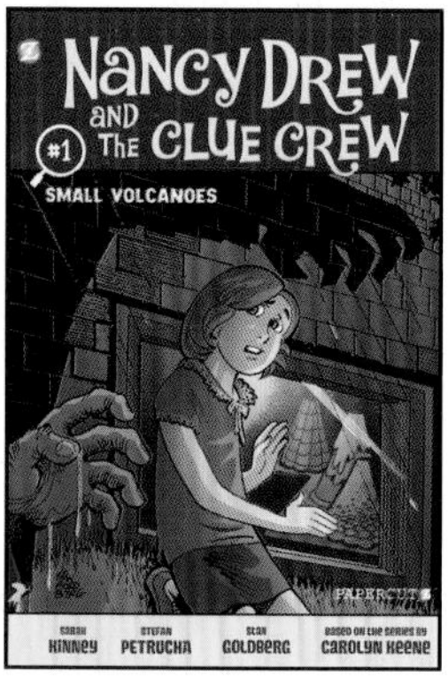
Nancy Drew and the Clue Crew
#1
SMALL VOLCANOES
PAPERCUTZ
SARAH KINNEY STEFAN PETRUCHA STAN GOLDBERG BASED ON THE SERIES BY CAROLYN KEENE

NANCY DREW AND THE CLUE CREW #1 "Small Volcanoes"

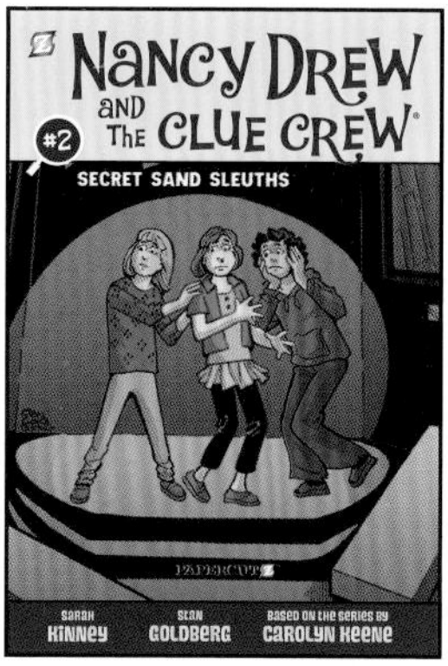
Nancy Drew and the Clue Crew
#2
SECRET SAND SLEUTHS
PAPERCUTZ
SARAH KINNEY STAN GOLDBERG BASED ON THE SERIES BY CAROLYN KEENE

NANCY DREW AND THE CLUE CREW #2 "Secret Sand Sleuths"

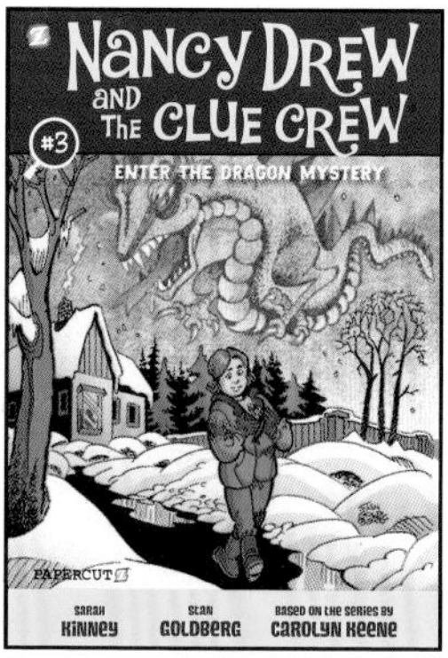
Nancy Drew and the Clue Crew
#3
ENTER THE DRAGON MYSTERY
PAPERCUTZ
SARAH KINNEY STAN GOLDBERG BASED ON THE SERIES BY CAROLYN KEENE

NANCY DREW AND THE CLUE CREW #3 "Enter the Dragon Mystery"

COMING SOON!

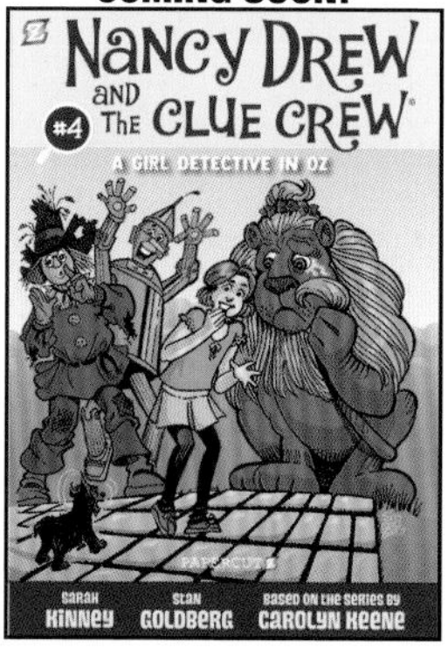
Nancy Drew and the Clue Crew
#4
A GIRL DETECTIVE IN OZ
PAPERCUTZ
SARAH KINNEY STAN GOLDBERG BASED ON THE SERIES BY CAROLYN KEENE

NANCY DREW AND THE CLUE CREW #4 "A Girl Detective in Oz"

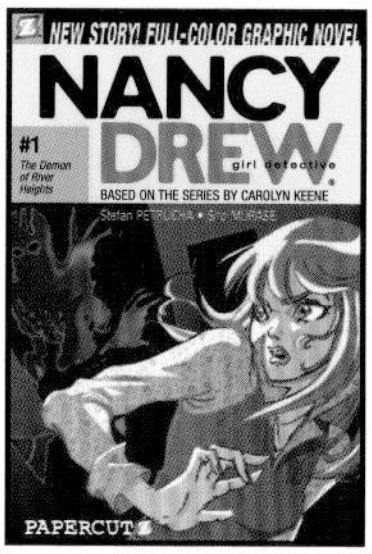
NEW STORY! FULL-COLOR GRAPHIC NOVEL
NANCY DREW
girl detective
BASED ON THE SERIES BY CAROLYN KEENE
PAPERCUTZ

#1 "The Demon of River Heights"

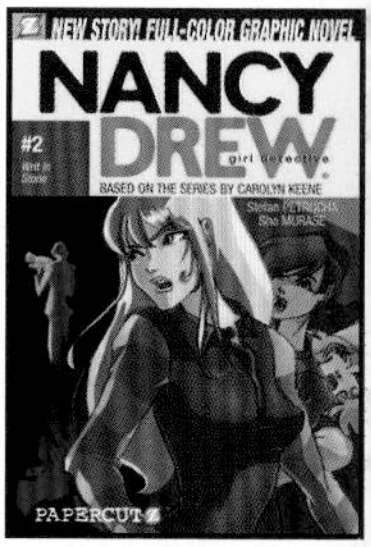
NEW STORY! FULL-COLOR GRAPHIC NOVEL
NANCY DREW
girl detective
BASED ON THE SERIES BY CAROLYN KEENE
PAPERCUTZ

#2 "Writ In Stone"

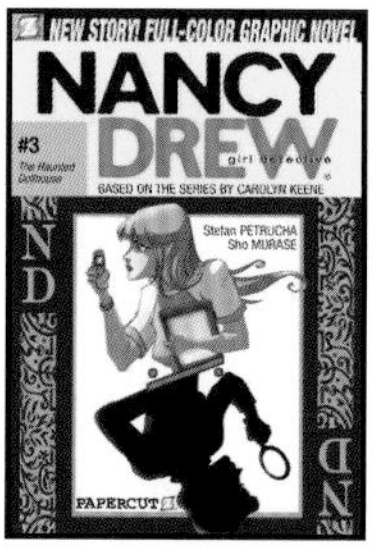
NEW STORY! FULL-COLOR GRAPHIC NOVEL
NANCY DREW
girl detective
BASED ON THE SERIES BY CAROLYN KEENE
PAPERCUTZ

#3 "The Haunted Dollhouse"

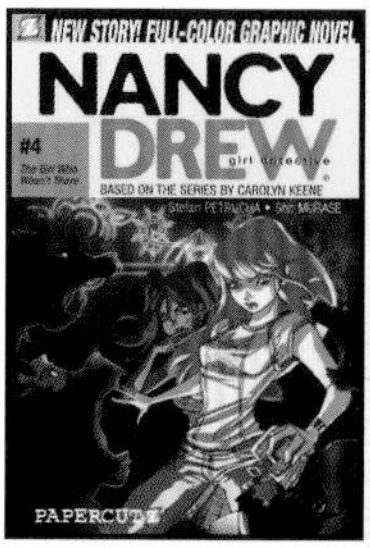
NEW STORY! FULL-COLOR GRAPHIC NOVEL
NANCY DREW
girl detective
BASED ON THE SERIES BY CAROLYN KEENE
PAPERCUTZ

#4 "The Girl Who Wasn't There"

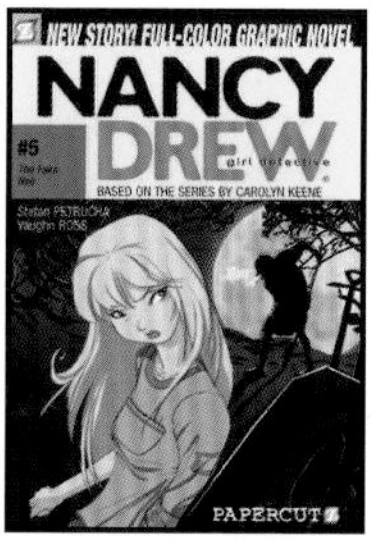
NEW STORY! FULL-COLOR GRAPHIC NOVEL
NANCY DREW
girl detective
BASED ON THE SERIES BY CAROLYN KEENE
PAPERCUTZ

#5 "The Fake Heir"

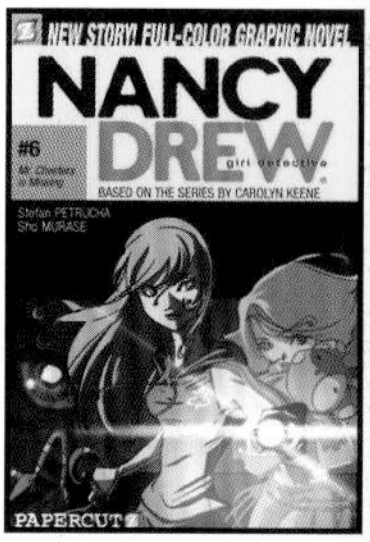
NEW STORY! FULL-COLOR GRAPHIC NOVEL
NANCY DREW
girl detective
BASED ON THE SERIES BY CAROLYN KEENE
PAPERCUTZ

#6 "Mr. Cheeters Is Missing"

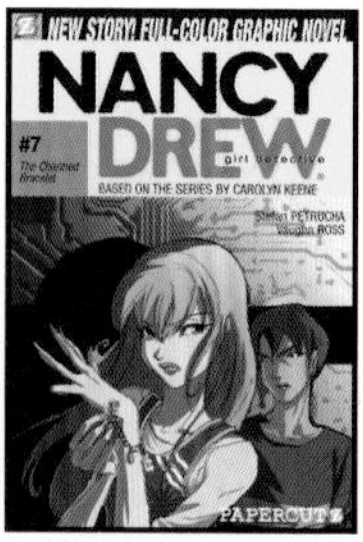
NEW STORY! FULL-COLOR GRAPHIC NOVEL
NANCY DREW
girl detective
BASED ON THE SERIES BY CAROLYN KEENE
PAPERCUTZ

#7 "The Charmed Bracelet"

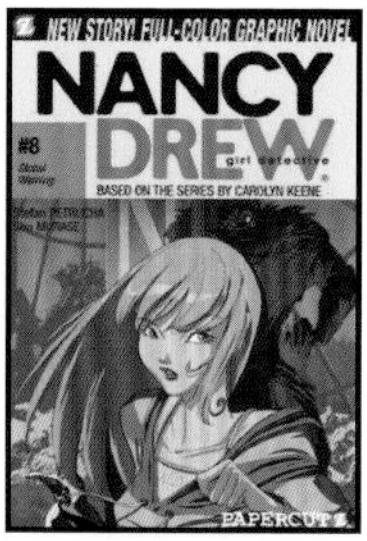
NEW STORY! FULL-COLOR GRAPHIC NOVEL
NANCY DREW
girl detective
BASED ON THE SERIES BY CAROLYN KEENE
PAPERCUTZ

#8 "Global Warning"

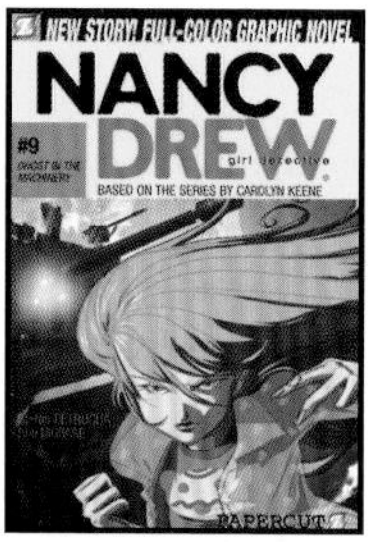
NEW STORY! FULL-COLOR GRAPHIC NOVEL
NANCY DREW
girl detective
BASED ON THE SERIES BY CAROLYN KEENE
PAPERCUTZ

#9 "Ghost In The Machinery"

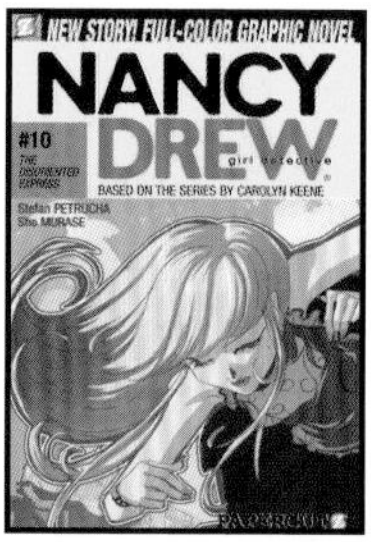
NEW STORY! FULL-COLOR GRAPHIC NOVEL
NANCY DREW
girl detective
BASED ON THE SERIES BY CAROLYN KEENE
PAPERCUTZ

#10 "The Disoriented Express"

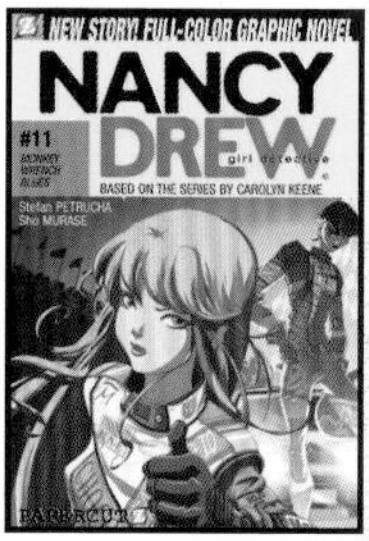
NEW STORY! FULL-COLOR GRAPHIC NOVEL
NANCY DREW
girl detective
BASED ON THE SERIES BY CAROLYN KEENE
PAPERCUTZ

#11 "Monkey Wrench Blues"

See page 55 for more NANCY DREW graphic novels!

NANCY DREW graphic novels are available at booksellers everywhere.

NANCY DREW graphic novels are $7.95 each in paperback and $12.95 each in hardcover. NANCY DREW AND THE CLUE CREW graphic novels are $7.99 each in paperback, and $11.99 each in hardcover, except #1, which is $6.99 in paperback; $10.99 in hardcover. You can also order online at www.papercutz.com. Or call 1-800-886-1223, Monday through Friday, 9 – 5 EST. MC, Visa, and AmEx accepted. To order by mail, please add $4.00 for postage and handling for first book ordered, $1.00 for each additional book and make check payable to NBM Publishing.

Send to: Papercutz, 160 Broadway, Suite 700, East Wing, New York, NY 10038.

NANCY DREW and NANCY DREW AND THE CLUE CREW graphic novels are also available digitally wherever e-books are sold.

www.papercutz.com

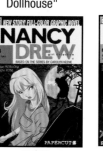

Nancy Drew and the Clue Crew

#3

Enter the Dragon Mystery

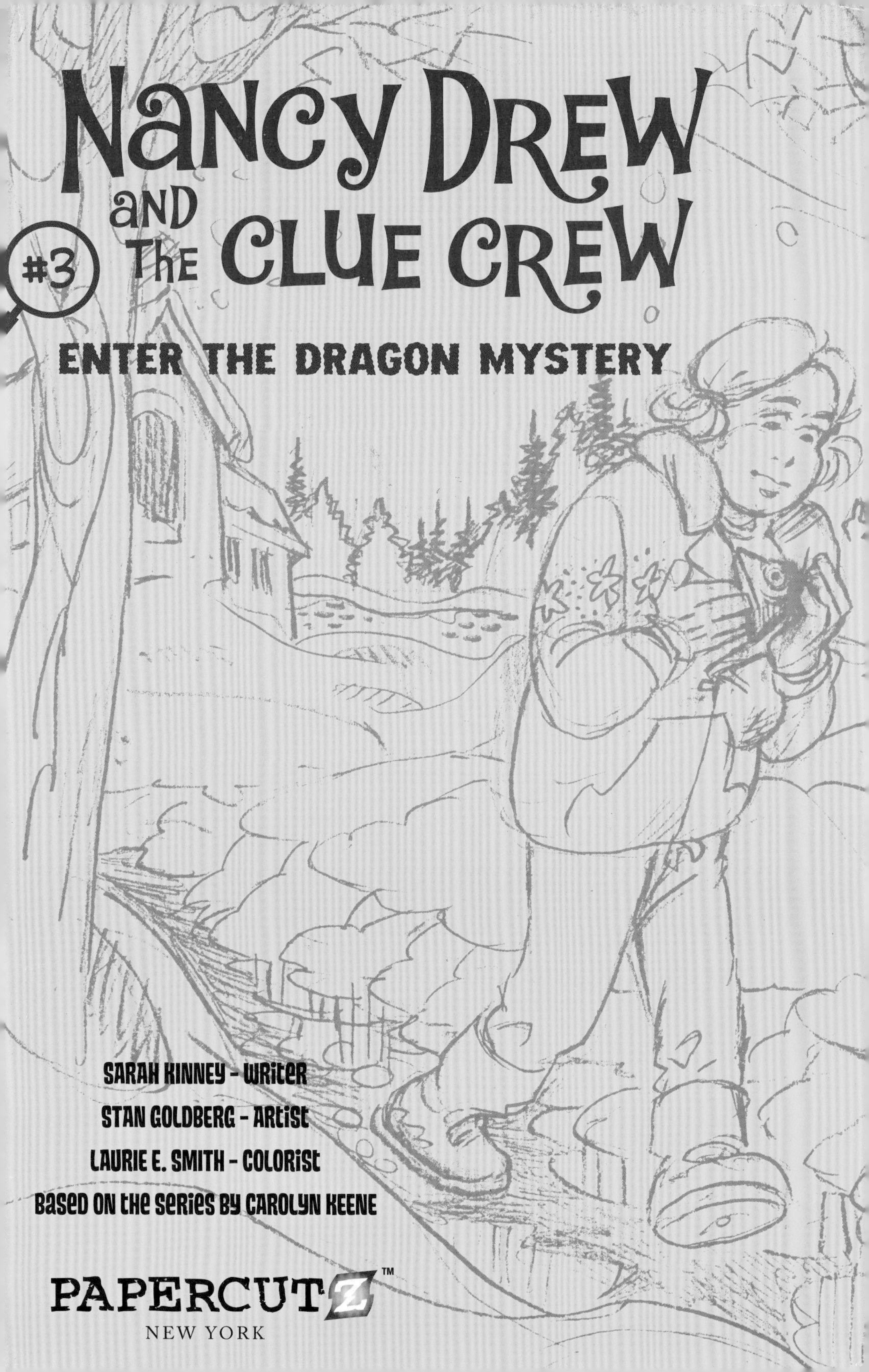

Sarah Kinney - Writer
Stan Goldberg - Artist
Laurie E. Smith - Colorist
Based on the series by Carolyn Keene

PAPERCUTZ™
NEW YORK

Nancy Drew and the Clue Crew
#3 "Enter the Dragon Mystery"
Sarah Kinney – Writer
Stan Goldberg – Artist
Laurie E. Smith – Colorist
Tom Orzechowski – Letterer
Production – Nelson Design Group, LLC
Beth Scorzato – Production Coordinator
Michael Petranek – Associate Editor
Jim Salicrup
Editor-in-Chief

ISBN: 978-1-59707-437-7 paperback edition
ISBN: 978-1-59707-438-4 hardcover edition

Printed in China
October 2013 by Asia One Printing, LTD
13/F Asia One Tower
8 Fung Yip St., Chaiwan, Hong Kong

Distributed by Macmillan

First Printing

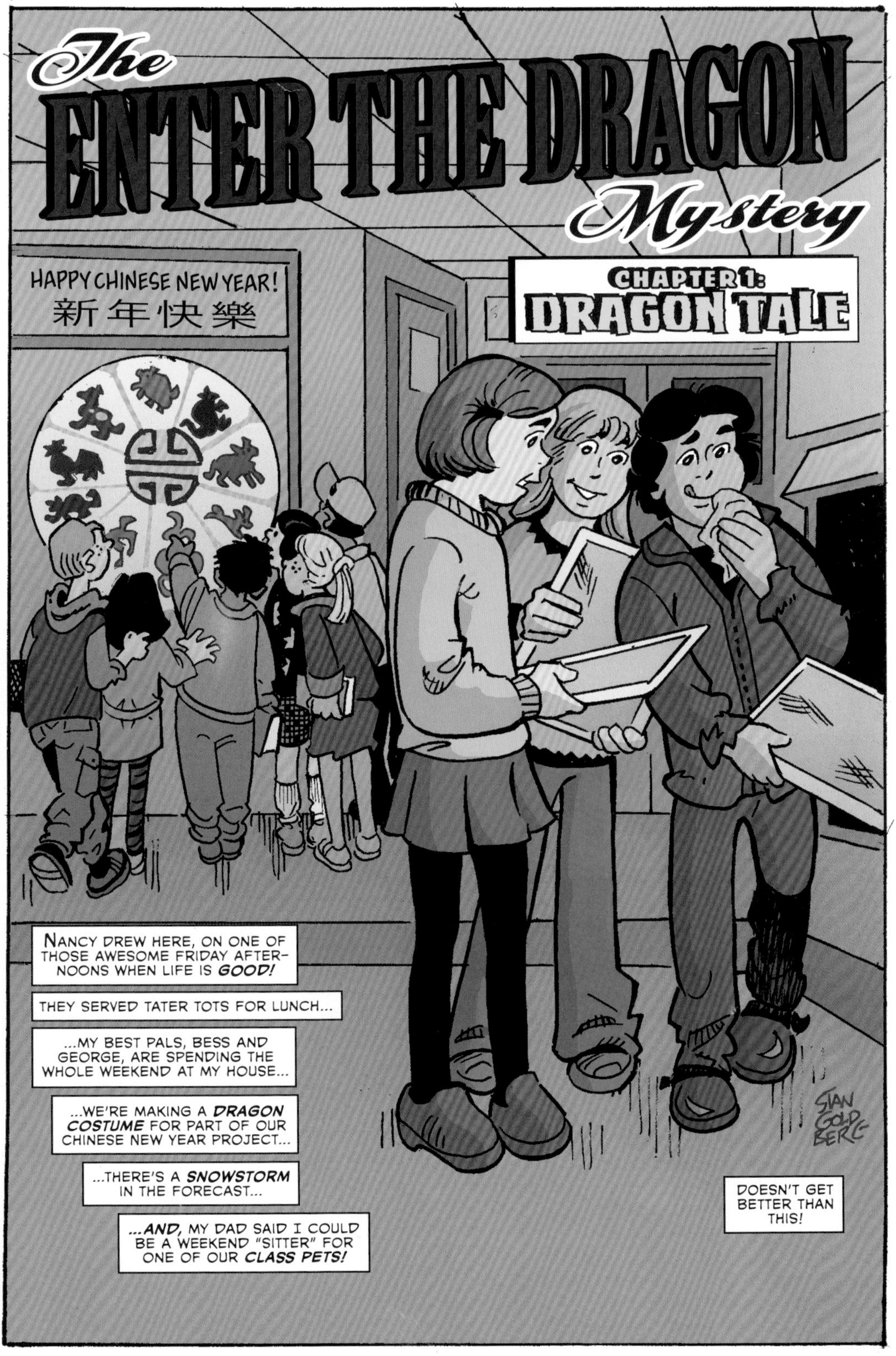

The ENTER THE DRAGON Mystery
CHAPTER 1: DRAGON TALE
HAPPY CHINESE NEW YEAR!
新年快樂
NANCY DREW HERE, ON ONE OF THOSE AWESOME FRIDAY AFTER-NOONS WHEN LIFE IS GOOD!
THEY SERVED TATER TOTS FOR LUNCH...
...MY BEST PALS, BESS AND GEORGE, ARE SPENDING THE WHOLE WEEKEND AT MY HOUSE...
...WE'RE MAKING A DRAGON COSTUME FOR PART OF OUR CHINESE NEW YEAR PROJECT...
...THERE'S A SNOWSTORM IN THE FORECAST...
...AND, MY DAD SAID I COULD BE A WEEKEND "SITTER" FOR ONE OF OUR CLASS PETS!
DOESN'T GET BETTER THAN THIS!
STAN GOLDBERG

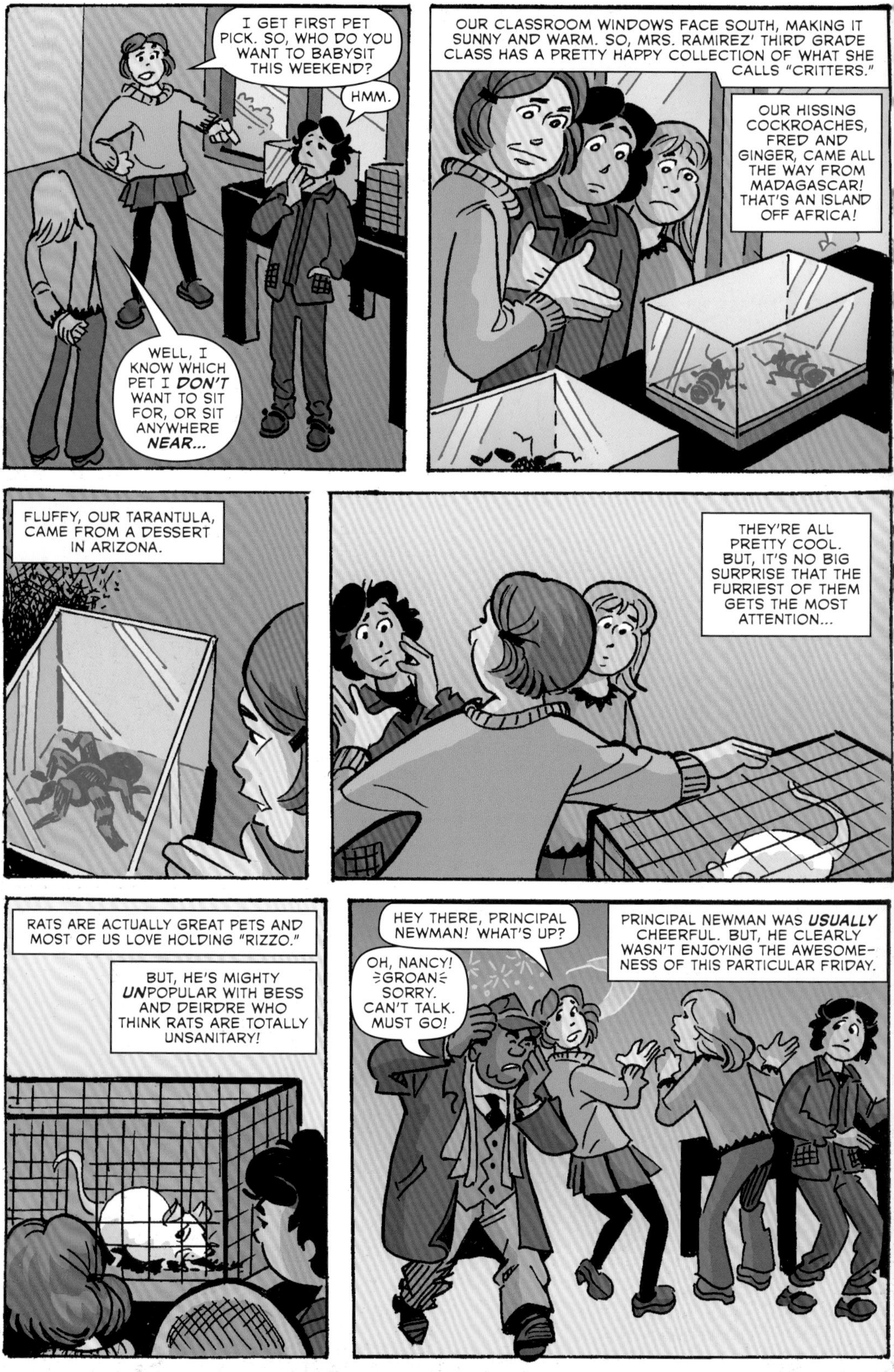
I GET FIRST PET PICK. SO, WHO DO YOU WANT TO BABYSIT THIS WEEKEND?
HMM.
WELL, I KNOW WHICH PET I DON'T WANT TO SIT FOR, OR SIT ANYWHERE NEAR...
OUR CLASSROOM WINDOWS FACE SOUTH, MAKING IT SUNNY AND WARM. SO, MRS. RAMIREZ' THIRD GRADE CLASS HAS A PRETTY HAPPY COLLECTION OF WHAT SHE CALLS "CRITTERS."
OUR HISSING COCKROACHES, FRED AND GINGER, CAME ALL THE WAY FROM MADAGASCAR! THAT'S AN ISLAND OFF AFRICA!
FLUFFY, OUR TARANTULA, CAME FROM A DESSERT IN ARIZONA.
THEY'RE ALL PRETTY COOL. BUT, IT'S NO BIG SURPRISE THAT THE FURRIEST OF THEM GETS THE MOST ATTENTION...
RATS ARE ACTUALLY GREAT PETS AND MOST OF US LOVE HOLDING "RIZZO."
BUT, HE'S MIGHTY UNPOPULAR WITH BESS AND DEIRDRE WHO THINK RATS ARE TOTALLY UNSANITARY!
HEY THERE, PRINCIPAL NEWMAN! WHAT'S UP?
PRINCIPAL NEWMAN WAS USUALLY CHEERFUL. BUT, HE CLEARLY WASN'T ENJOYING THE AWESOMENESS OF THIS PARTICULAR FRIDAY.
OH, NANCY! GROAN SORRY. CAN'T TALK. MUST GO!

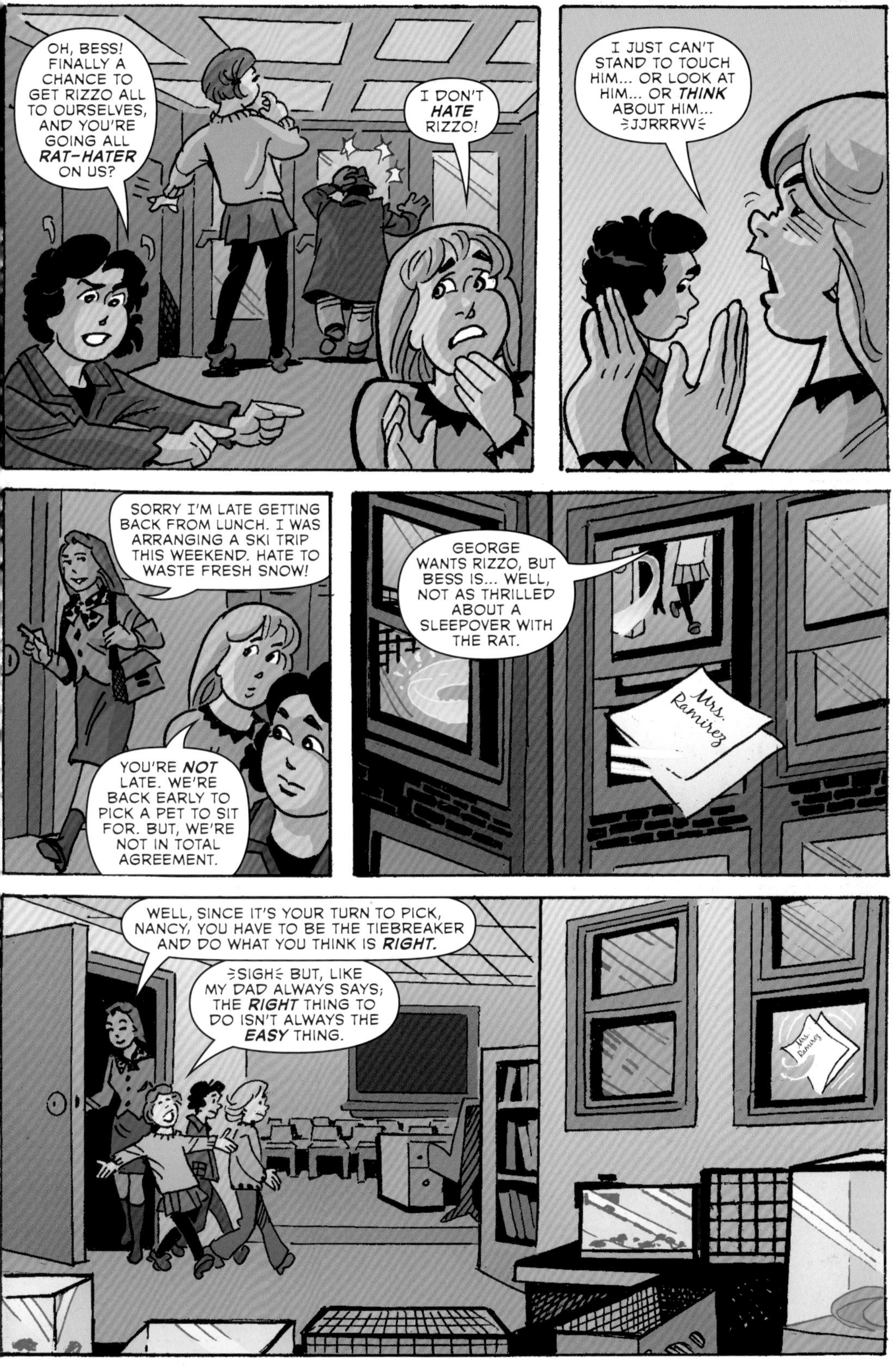
OH, BESS! FINALLY A CHANCE TO GET RIZZO ALL TO OURSELVES, AND YOU'RE GOING ALL *RAT-HATER* ON US?
I DON'T *HATE* RIZZO!
I JUST CAN'T STAND TO TOUCH HIM... OR LOOK AT HIM... OR *THINK* ABOUT HIM... ≶JJRRRW≶
SORRY I'M LATE GETTING BACK FROM LUNCH. I WAS ARRANGING A SKI TRIP THIS WEEKEND. HATE TO WASTE FRESH SNOW!
YOU'RE *NOT* LATE. WE'RE BACK EARLY TO PICK A PET TO SIT FOR. BUT, WE'RE NOT IN TOTAL AGREEMENT.
GEORGE WANTS RIZZO, BUT BESS IS... WELL, NOT AS THRILLED ABOUT A SLEEPOVER WITH THE RAT.
Mrs. Ramirez
WELL, SINCE IT'S YOUR TURN TO PICK, NANCY, YOU HAVE TO BE THE TIEBREAKER AND DO WHAT YOU THINK IS *RIGHT.*
≶SIGH≶ BUT, LIKE MY DAD ALWAYS SAYS; THE *RIGHT* THING TO DO ISN'T ALWAYS THE *EASY* THING.
Mrs. Ramirez

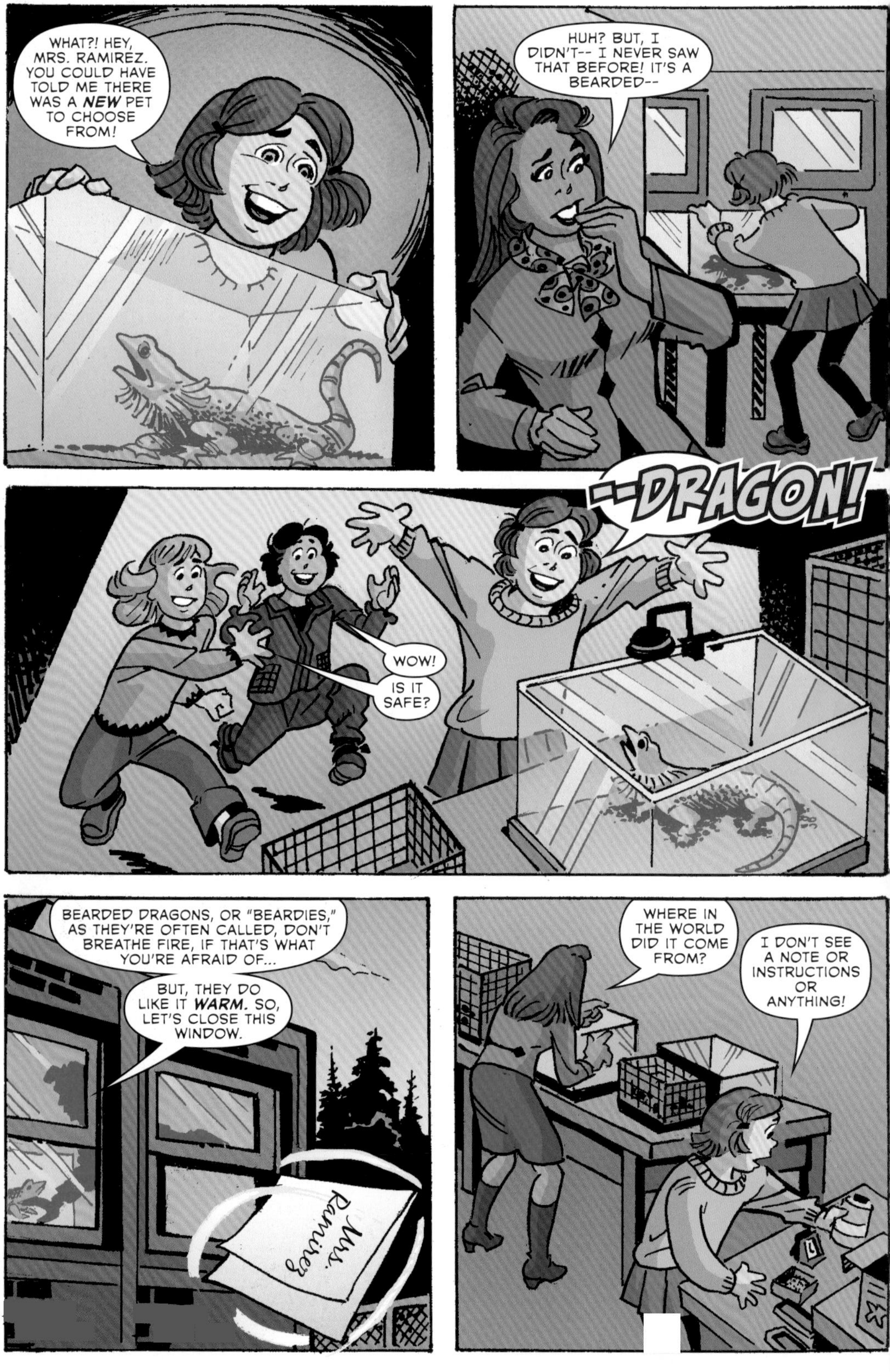
WHAT?! HEY, MRS. RAMIREZ. YOU COULD HAVE TOLD ME THERE WAS A *NEW* PET TO CHOOSE FROM!
HUH? BUT, I DIDN'T-- I NEVER SAW THAT BEFORE! IT'S A BEARDED--
--DRAGON!
WOW!
IS IT SAFE?
BEARDED DRAGONS, OR "BEARDIES," AS THEY'RE OFTEN CALLED, DON'T BREATHE FIRE, IF THAT'S WHAT YOU'RE AFRAID OF...
BUT, THEY DO LIKE IT **WARM.** SO, LET'S CLOSE THIS WINDOW.
Mrs. Ramirez
WHERE IN THE WORLD DID IT COME FROM?
I DON'T SEE A NOTE OR INSTRUCTIONS OR ANYTHING!

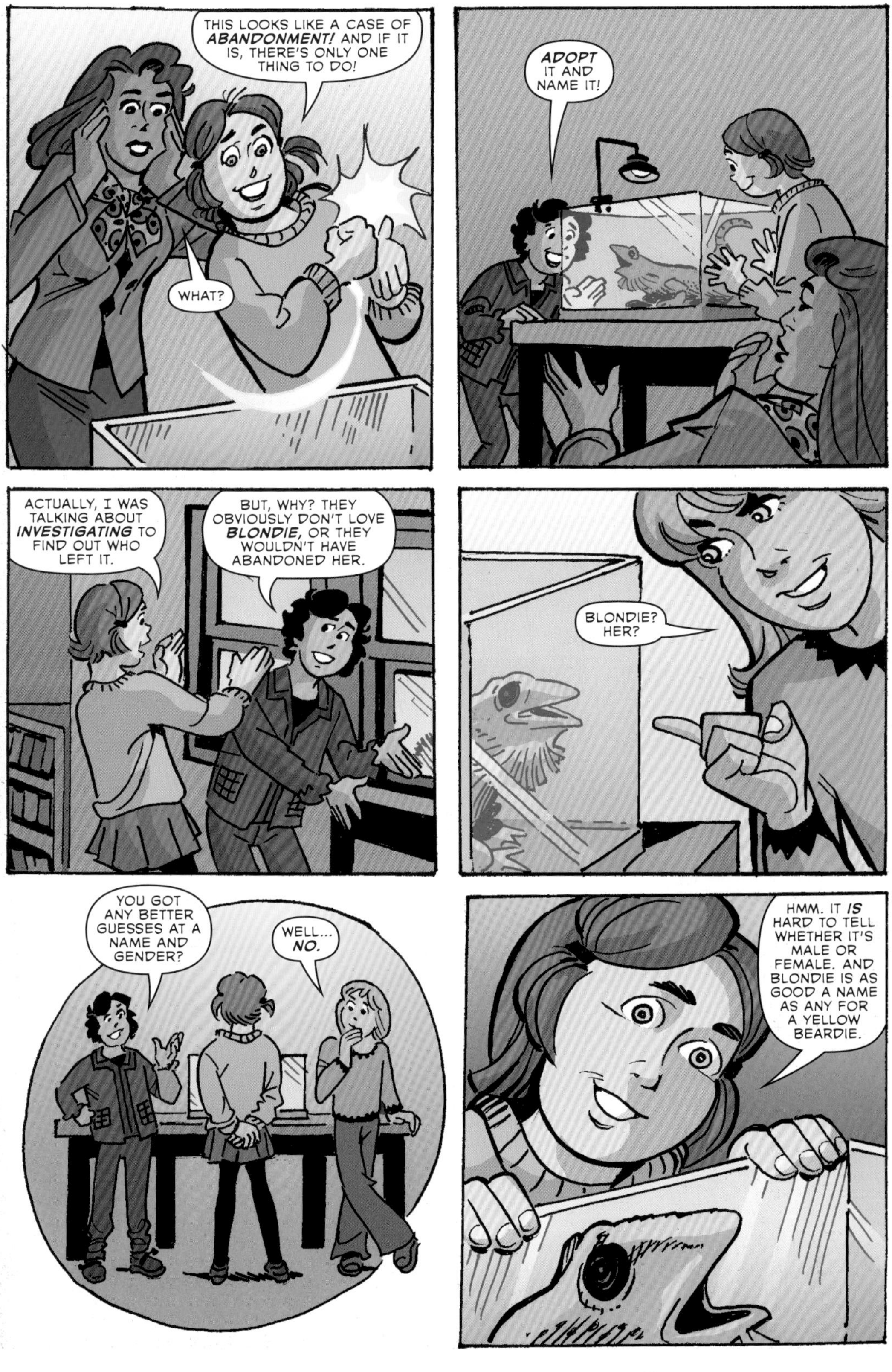
THIS LOOKS LIKE A CASE OF ABANDONMENT! AND IF IT IS, THERE'S ONLY ONE THING TO DO!
WHAT?
ADOPT IT AND NAME IT!
ACTUALLY, I WAS TALKING ABOUT INVESTIGATING TO FIND OUT WHO LEFT IT.
BUT, WHY? THEY OBVIOUSLY DON'T LOVE BLONDIE, OR THEY WOULDN'T HAVE ABANDONED HER.
BLONDIE? HER?
YOU GOT ANY BETTER GUESSES AT A NAME AND GENDER?
WELL... NO.
HMM. IT IS HARD TO TELL WHETHER IT'S MALE OR FEMALE. AND BLONDIE IS AS GOOD A NAME AS ANY FOR A YELLOW BEARDIE.

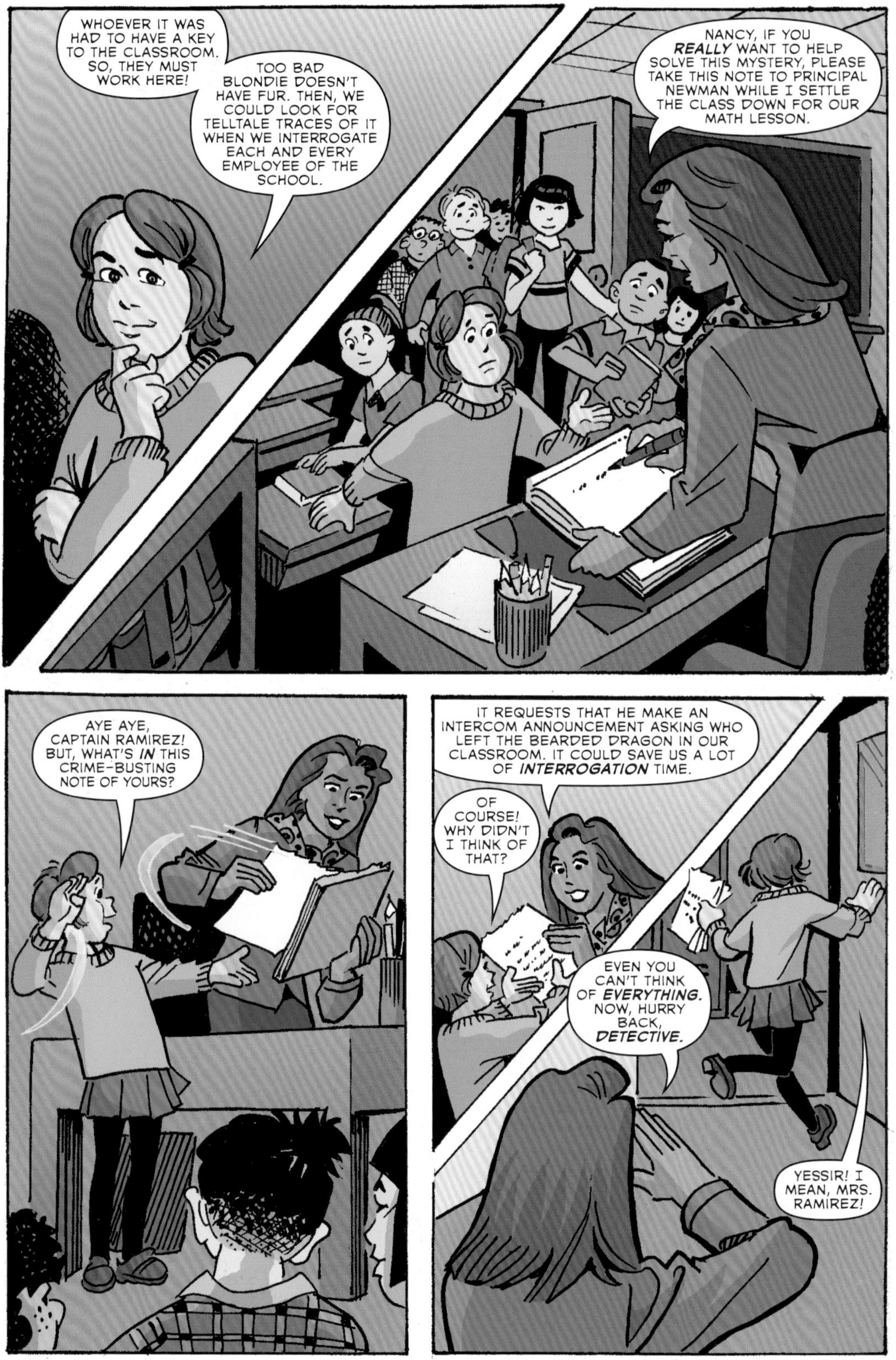
WHOEVER IT WAS HAD TO HAVE A KEY TO THE CLASSROOM. SO, THEY MUST WORK HERE!
TOO BAD BLONDIE DOESN'T HAVE FUR. THEN, WE COULD LOOK FOR TELLTALE TRACES OF IT WHEN WE INTERROGATE EACH AND EVERY EMPLOYEE OF THE SCHOOL.
NANCY, IF YOU **REALLY** WANT TO HELP SOLVE THIS MYSTERY, PLEASE TAKE THIS NOTE TO PRINCIPAL NEWMAN WHILE I SETTLE THE CLASS DOWN FOR OUR MATH LESSON.
AYE AYE, CAPTAIN RAMIREZ! BUT, WHAT'S **IN** THIS CRIME-BUSTING NOTE OF YOURS?
IT REQUESTS THAT HE MAKE AN INTERCOM ANNOUNCEMENT ASKING WHO LEFT THE BEARDED DRAGON IN OUR CLASSROOM. IT COULD SAVE US A LOT OF **INTERROGATION** TIME.
OF COURSE! WHY DIDN'T I THINK OF THAT?
EVEN YOU CAN'T THINK OF **EVERYTHING.** NOW, HURRY BACK, **DETECTIVE.**
YESSIR! I MEAN, MRS. RAMIREZ!

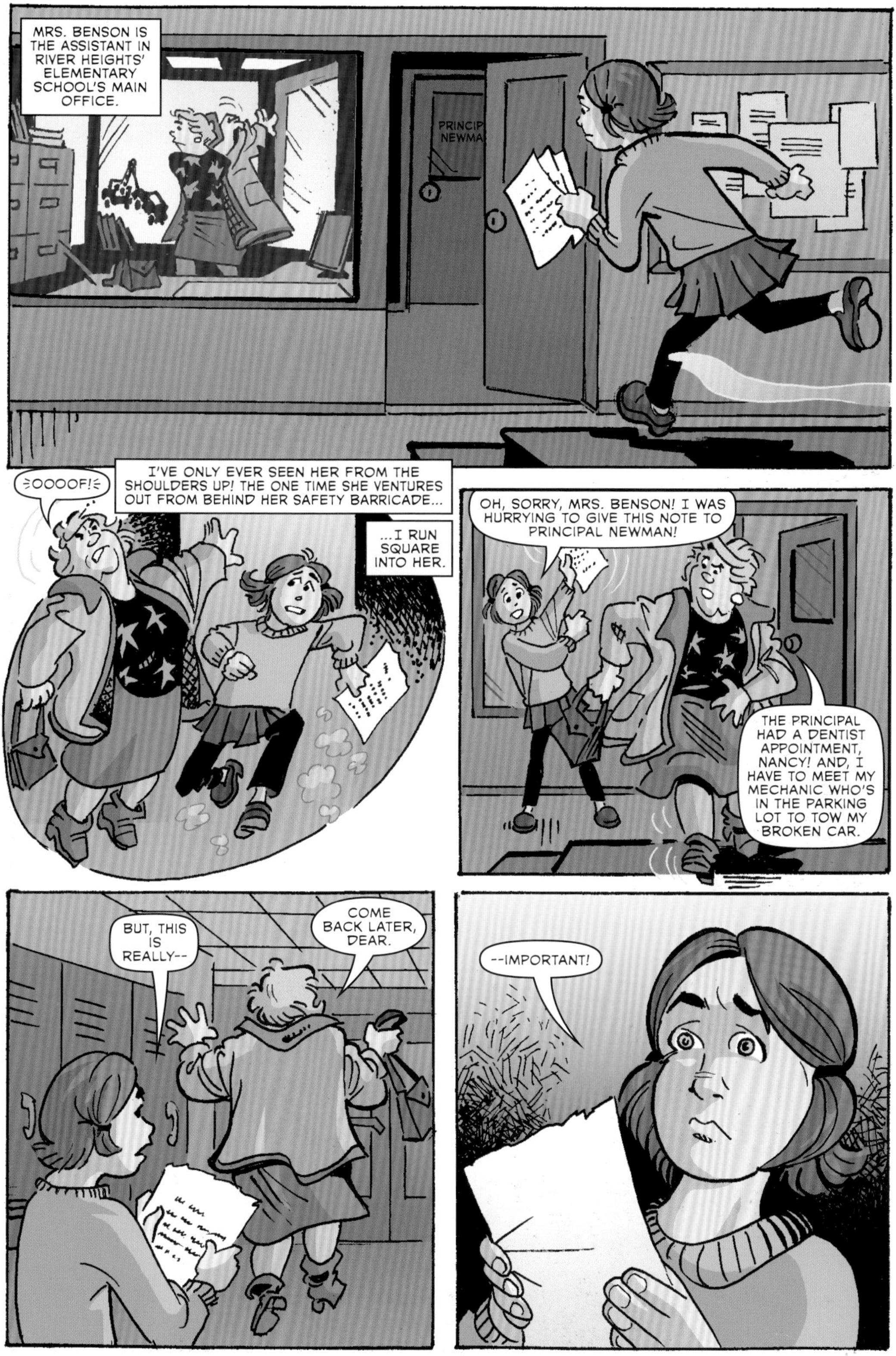
MRS. BENSON IS THE ASSISTANT IN RIVER HEIGHTS' ELEMENTARY SCHOOL'S MAIN OFFICE.
PRINCIP
NEWMA
OOOOF!
I'VE ONLY EVER SEEN HER FROM THE SHOULDERS UP! THE ONE TIME SHE VENTURES OUT FROM BEHIND HER SAFETY BARRICADE...
...I RUN SQUARE INTO HER.
OH, SORRY, MRS. BENSON! I WAS HURRYING TO GIVE THIS NOTE TO PRINCIPAL NEWMAN!
THE PRINCIPAL HAD A DENTIST APPOINTMENT, NANCY! AND, I HAVE TO MEET MY MECHANIC WHO'S IN THE PARKING LOT TO TOW MY BROKEN CAR.
BUT, THIS IS REALLY--
COME BACK LATER, DEAR.
--IMPORTANT!

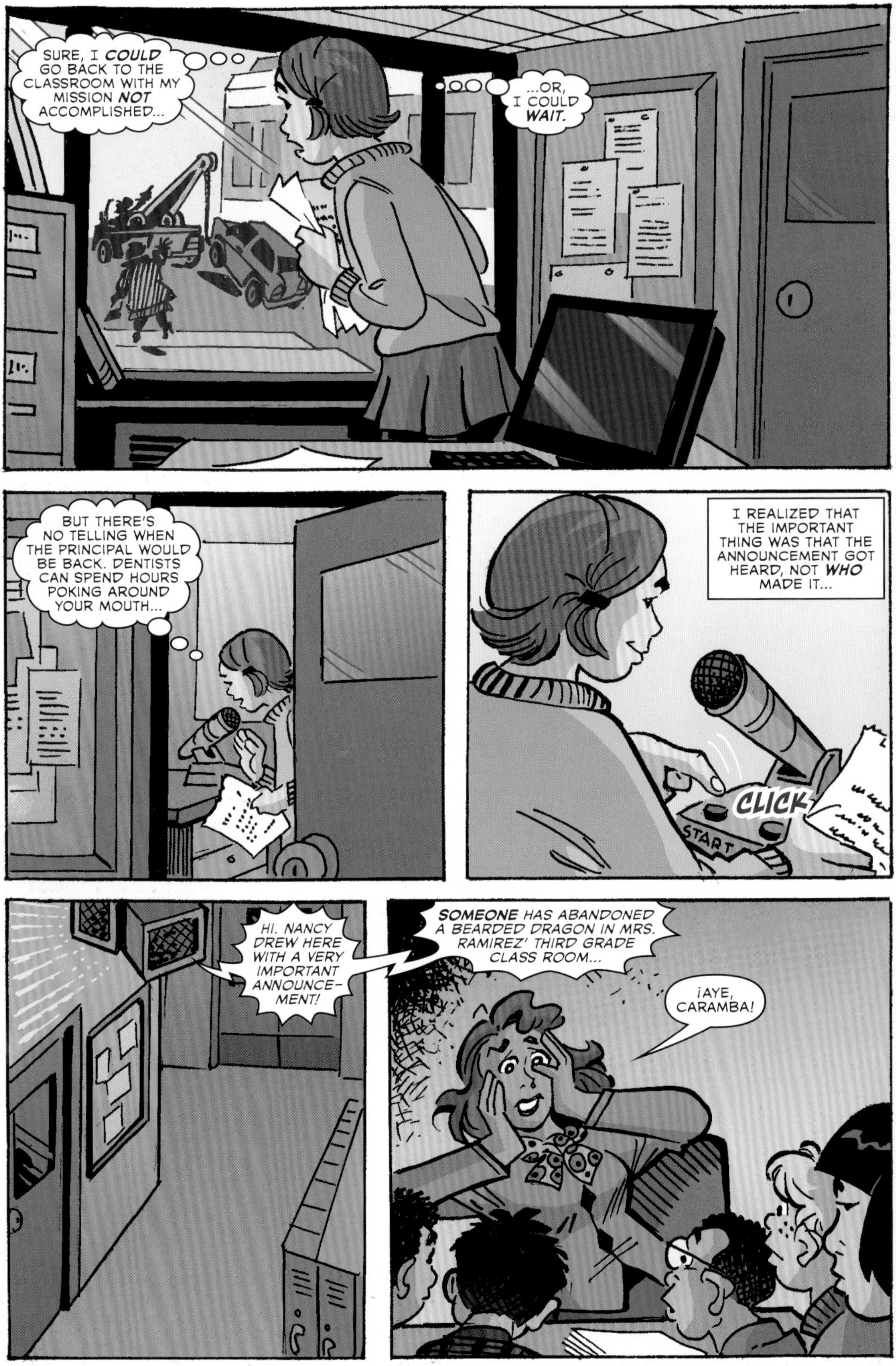
SURE, I COULD GO BACK TO THE CLASSROOM WITH MY MISSION NOT ACCOMPLISHED...
...OR, I COULD WAIT.
BUT THERE'S NO TELLING WHEN THE PRINCIPAL WOULD BE BACK. DENTISTS CAN SPEND HOURS POKING AROUND YOUR MOUTH...
I REALIZED THAT THE IMPORTANT THING WAS THAT THE ANNOUNCEMENT GOT HEARD, NOT WHO MADE IT...
CLICK
START
HI. NANCY DREW HERE WITH A VERY IMPORTANT ANNOUNCE-MENT!
SOMEONE HAS ABANDONED A BEARDED DRAGON IN MRS. RAMIREZ' THIRD GRADE CLASS ROOM...
¡AYE, CARAMBA!

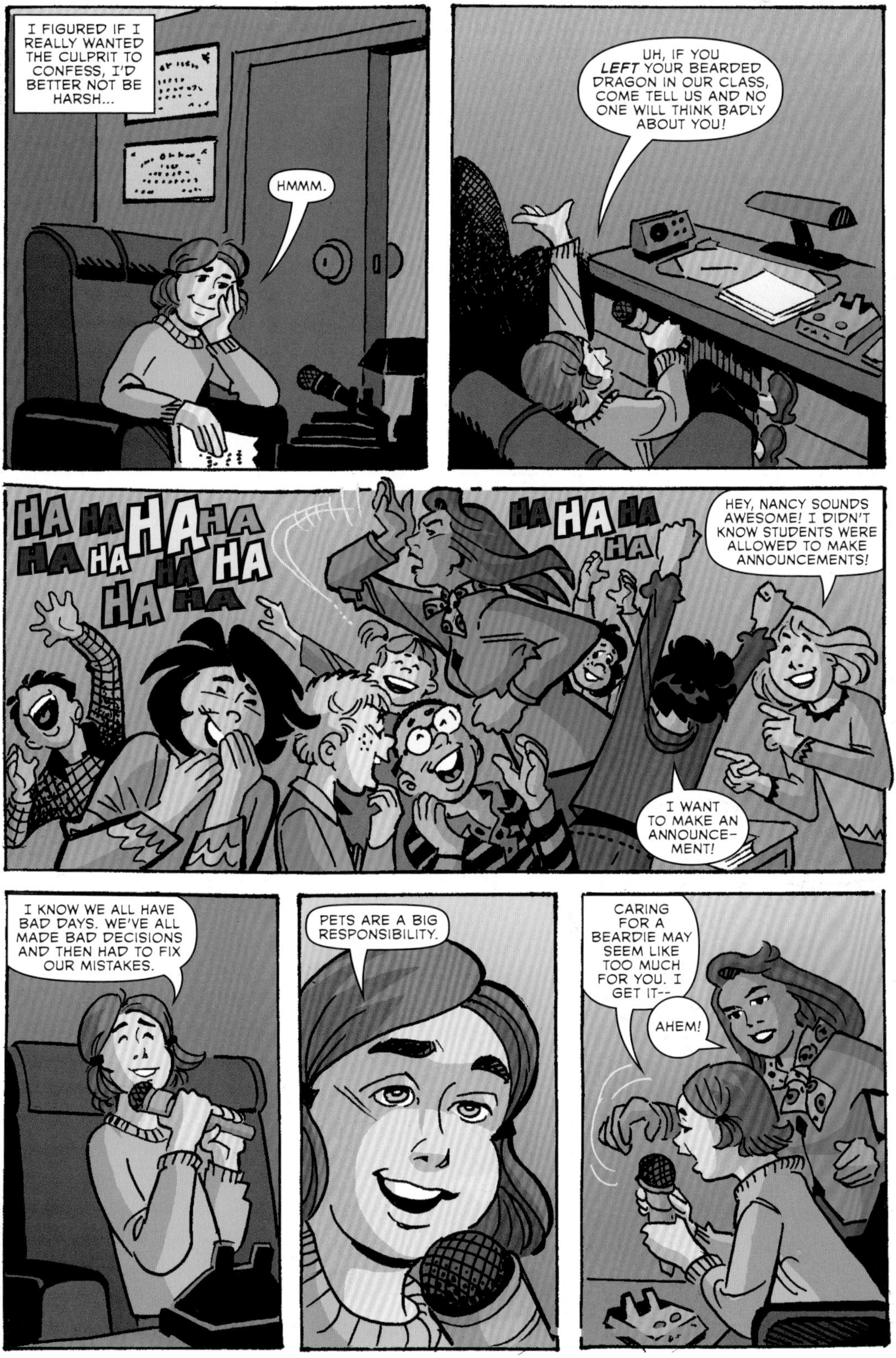
I FIGURED IF I REALLY WANTED THE CULPRIT TO CONFESS, I'D BETTER NOT BE HARSH...
HMMM.
UH, IF YOU LEFT YOUR BEARDED DRAGON IN OUR CLASS, COME TELL US AND NO ONE WILL THINK BADLY ABOUT YOU!
HA HA HA HA HA HA HA HA HA HA HA HA
HA HA HA HA
HEY, NANCY SOUNDS AWESOME! I DIDN'T KNOW STUDENTS WERE ALLOWED TO MAKE ANNOUNCEMENTS!
I WANT TO MAKE AN ANNOUNCE-MENT!
I KNOW WE ALL HAVE BAD DAYS. WE'VE ALL MADE BAD DECISIONS AND THEN HAD TO FIX OUR MISTAKES.
PETS ARE A BIG RESPONSIBILITY.
CARING FOR A BEARDIE MAY SEEM LIKE TOO MUCH FOR YOU. I GET IT--
AHEM!

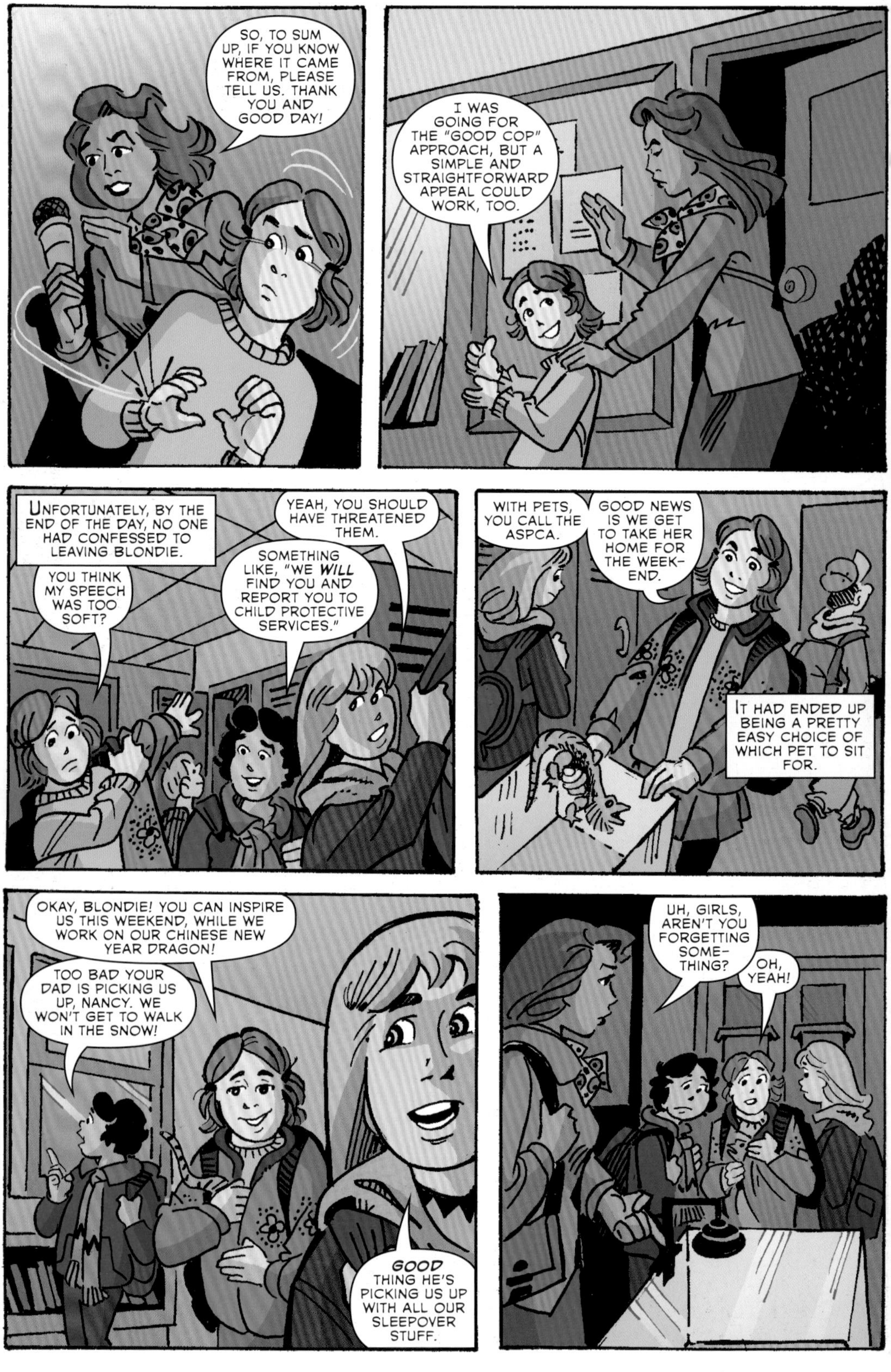
SO, TO SUM UP, IF YOU KNOW WHERE IT CAME FROM, PLEASE TELL US. THANK YOU AND GOOD DAY!
I WAS GOING FOR THE "GOOD COP" APPROACH, BUT A SIMPLE AND STRAIGHTFORWARD APPEAL COULD WORK, TOO.
UNFORTUNATELY, BY THE END OF THE DAY, NO ONE HAD CONFESSED TO LEAVING BLONDIE.
YOU THINK MY SPEECH WAS TOO SOFT?
YEAH, YOU SHOULD HAVE THREATENED THEM.
SOMETHING LIKE, "WE WILL FIND YOU AND REPORT YOU TO CHILD PROTECTIVE SERVICES."
WITH PETS, YOU CALL THE ASPCA.
GOOD NEWS IS WE GET TO TAKE HER HOME FOR THE WEEK-END.
IT HAD ENDED UP BEING A PRETTY EASY CHOICE OF WHICH PET TO SIT FOR.
OKAY, BLONDIE! YOU CAN INSPIRE US THIS WEEKEND, WHILE WE WORK ON OUR CHINESE NEW YEAR DRAGON!
TOO BAD YOUR DAD IS PICKING US UP, NANCY. WE WON'T GET TO WALK IN THE SNOW!
GOOD THING HE'S PICKING US UP WITH ALL OUR SLEEPOVER STUFF.
UH, GIRLS, AREN'T YOU FORGETTING SOME-THING?
OH, YEAH!

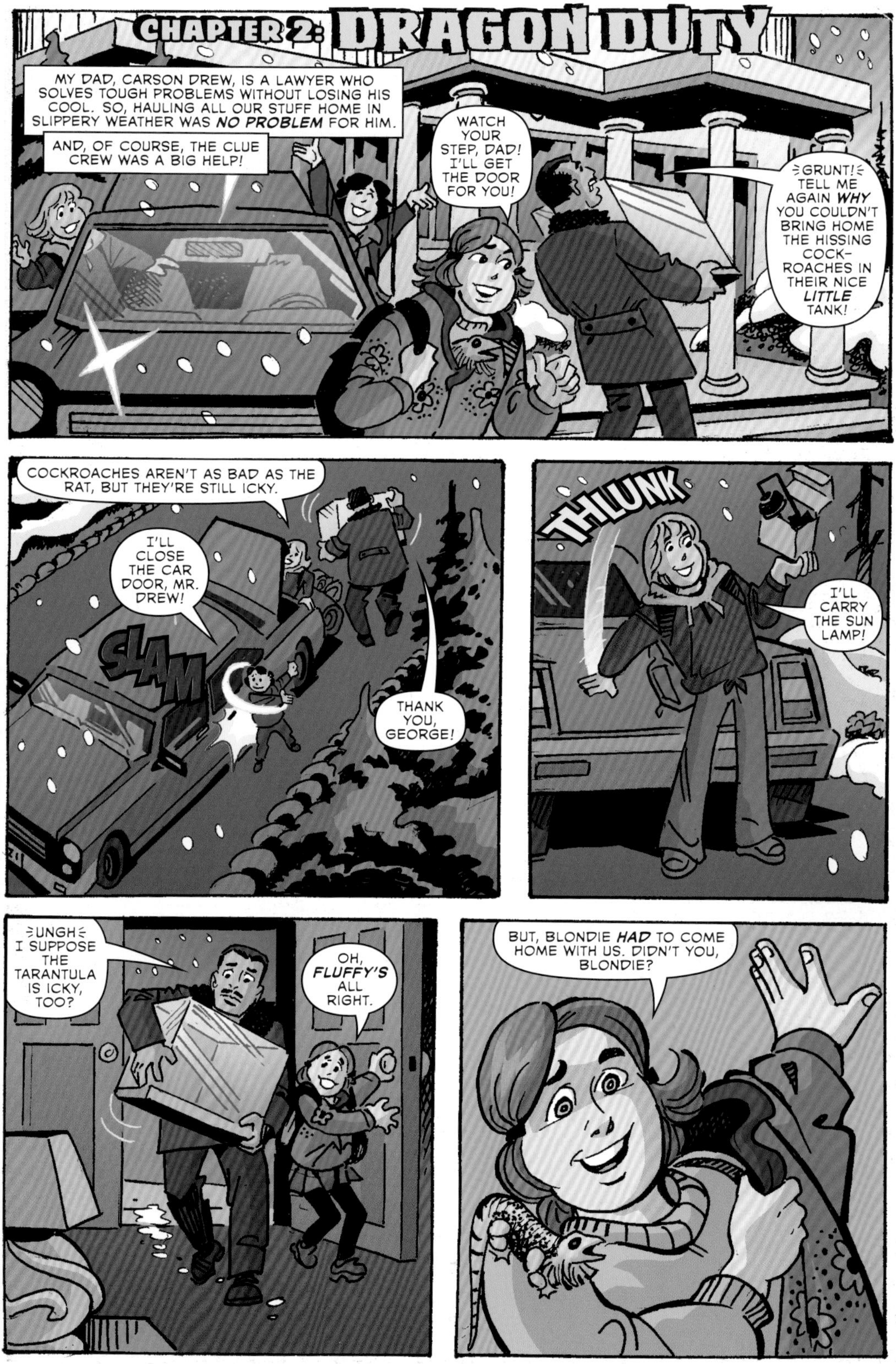
CHAPTER 2: DRAGON DUTY
MY DAD, CARSON DREW, IS A LAWYER WHO SOLVES TOUGH PROBLEMS WITHOUT LOSING HIS COOL. SO, HAULING ALL OUR STUFF HOME IN SLIPPERY WEATHER WAS NO PROBLEM FOR HIM.
AND, OF COURSE, THE CLUE CREW WAS A BIG HELP!
WATCH YOUR STEP, DAD! I'LL GET THE DOOR FOR YOU!
GRUNT! TELL ME AGAIN WHY YOU COULDN'T BRING HOME THE HISSING COCK-ROACHES IN THEIR NICE LITTLE TANK!
COCKROACHES AREN'T AS BAD AS THE RAT, BUT THEY'RE STILL ICKY.
I'LL CLOSE THE CAR DOOR, MR. DREW!
SLAM
THANK YOU, GEORGE!
THLUNK
I'LL CARRY THE SUN LAMP!
UNGH I SUPPOSE THE TARANTULA IS ICKY, TOO?
OH, FLUFFY'S ALL RIGHT.
BUT, BLONDIE HAD TO COME HOME WITH US. DIDN'T YOU, BLONDIE?

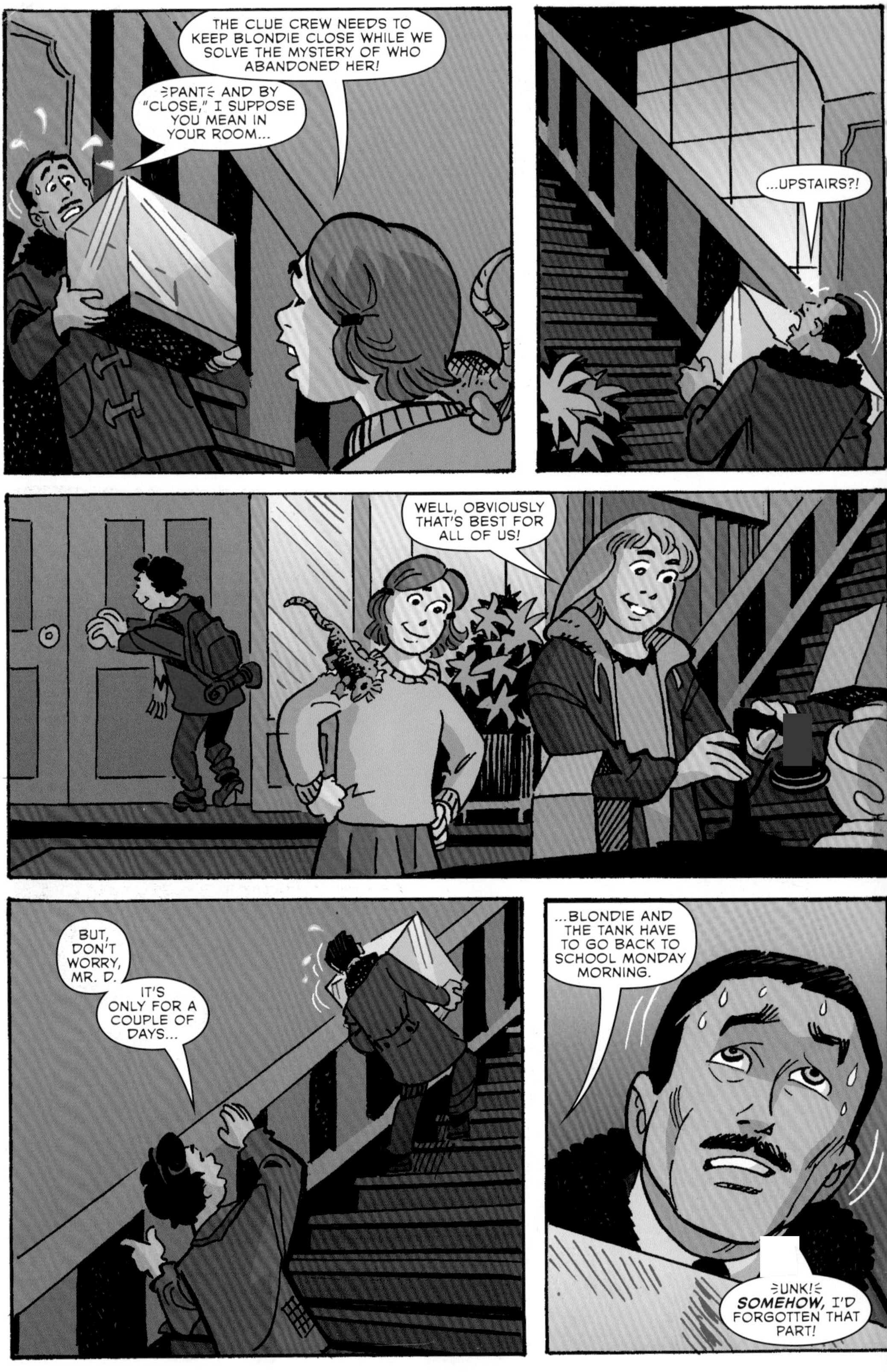
THE CLUE CREW NEEDS TO KEEP BLONDIE CLOSE WHILE WE SOLVE THE MYSTERY OF WHO ABANDONED HER!
≥PANT≤ AND BY "CLOSE," I SUPPOSE YOU MEAN IN YOUR ROOM...
...UPSTAIRS?!
WELL, OBVIOUSLY THAT'S BEST FOR ALL OF US!
BUT, DON'T WORRY, MR. D.
IT'S ONLY FOR A COUPLE OF DAYS...
...BLONDIE AND THE TANK HAVE TO GO BACK TO SCHOOL MONDAY MORNING.
≥UNK!≤ *SOMEHOW,* I'D FORGOTTEN THAT PART!

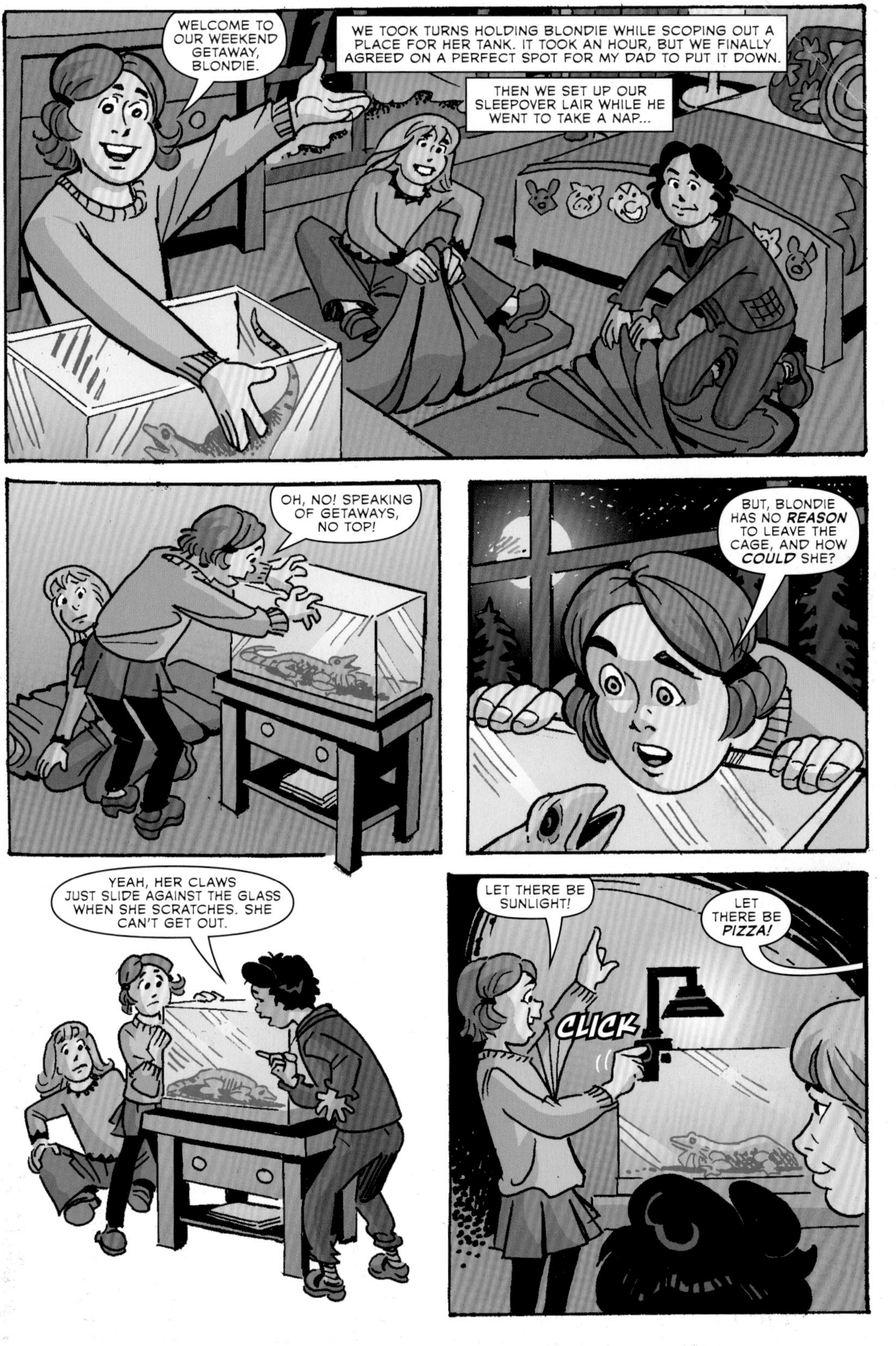
WELCOME TO OUR WEEKEND GETAWAY, BLONDIE.
WE TOOK TURNS HOLDING BLONDIE WHILE SCOPING OUT A PLACE FOR HER TANK. IT TOOK AN HOUR, BUT WE FINALLY AGREED ON A PERFECT SPOT FOR MY DAD TO PUT IT DOWN.
THEN WE SET UP OUR SLEEPOVER LAIR WHILE HE WENT TO TAKE A NAP...
OH, NO! SPEAKING OF GETAWAYS, NO TOP!
BUT, BLONDIE HAS NO REASON TO LEAVE THE CAGE, AND HOW COULD SHE?
YEAH, HER CLAWS JUST SLIDE AGAINST THE GLASS WHEN SHE SCRATCHES. SHE CAN'T GET OUT.
LET THERE BE SUNLIGHT!
LET THERE BE PIZZA!
CLICK

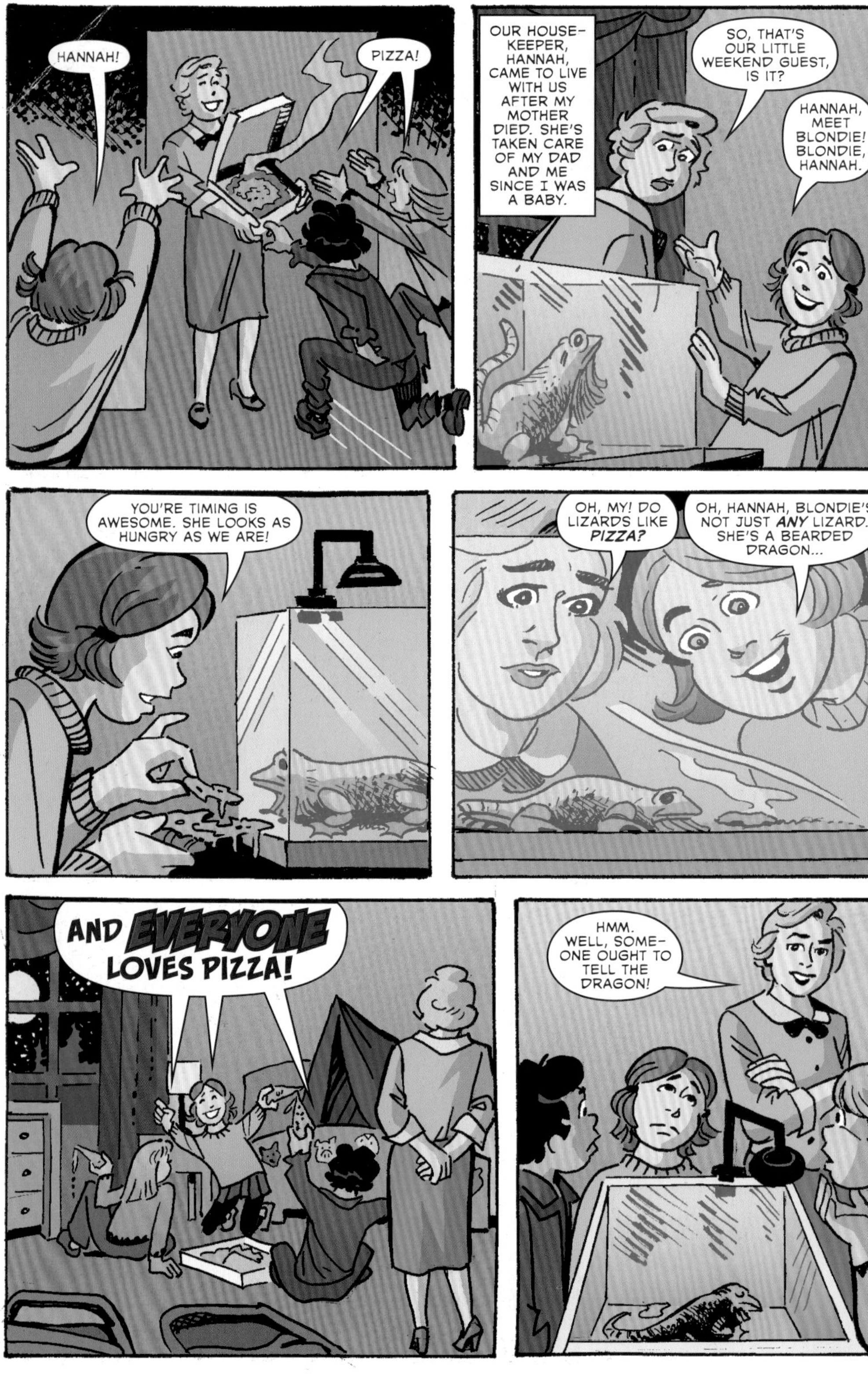
HANNAH!
PIZZA!
OUR HOUSE-KEEPER, HANNAH, CAME TO LIVE WITH US AFTER MY MOTHER DIED. SHE'S TAKEN CARE OF MY DAD AND ME SINCE I WAS A BABY.
SO, THAT'S OUR LITTLE WEEKEND GUEST, IS IT?
HANNAH, MEET BLONDIE! BLONDIE, HANNAH.
YOU'RE TIMING IS AWESOME. SHE LOOKS AS HUNGRY AS WE ARE!
OH, MY! DO LIZARDS LIKE *PIZZA?*
OH, HANNAH, BLONDIE'S NOT JUST *ANY* LIZARD. SHE'S A BEARDED DRAGON...
AND EVERYONE LOVES PIZZA!
HMM. WELL, SOME-ONE OUGHT TO TELL THE DRAGON!

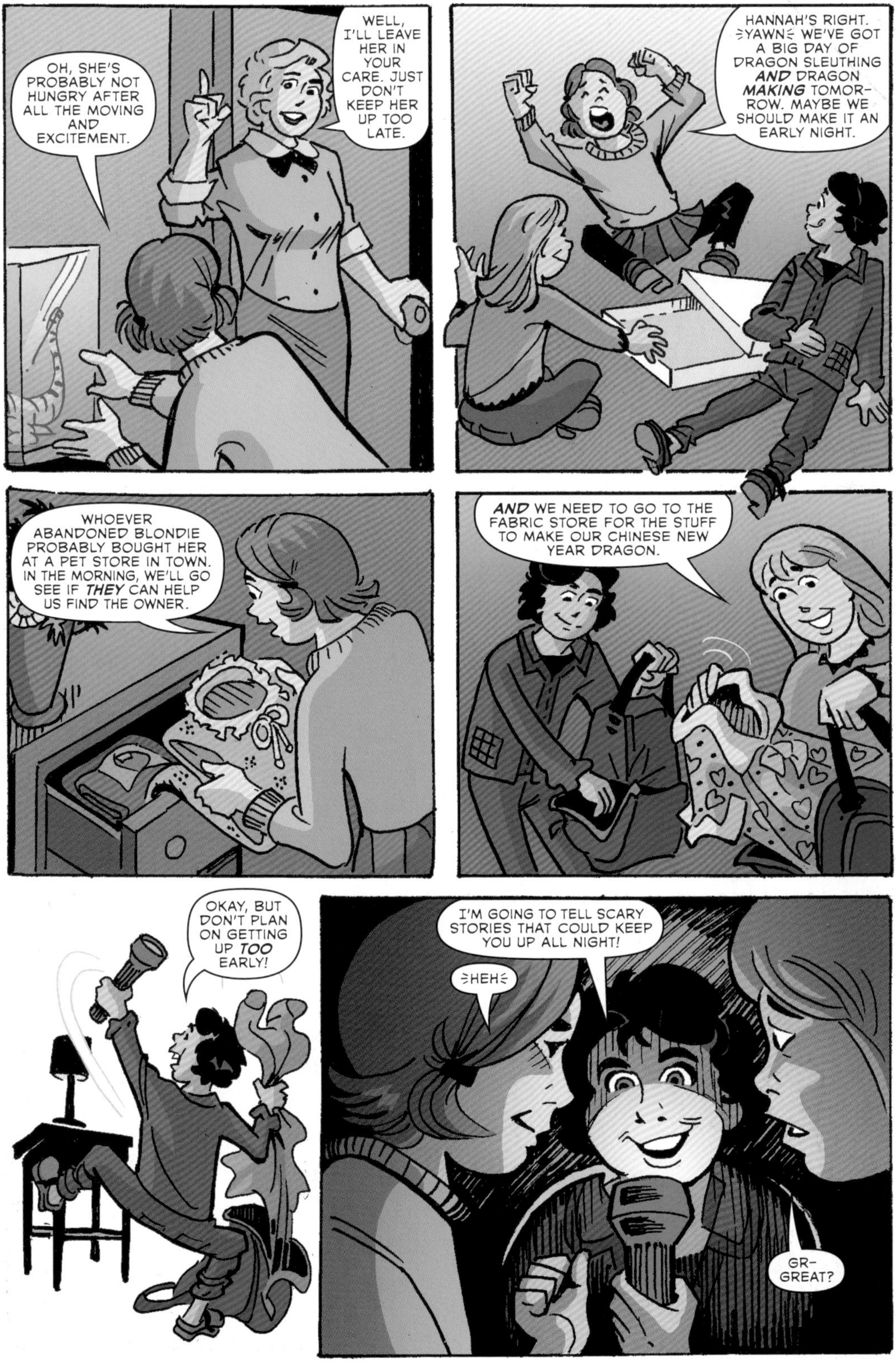
OH, SHE'S PROBABLY NOT HUNGRY AFTER ALL THE MOVING AND EXCITEMENT.
WELL, I'LL LEAVE HER IN YOUR CARE. JUST DON'T KEEP HER UP TOO LATE.
HANNAH'S RIGHT. YAWN WE'VE GOT A BIG DAY OF DRAGON SLEUTHING AND DRAGON MAKING TOMORROW. MAYBE WE SHOULD MAKE IT AN EARLY NIGHT.
WHOEVER ABANDONED BLONDIE PROBABLY BOUGHT HER AT A PET STORE IN TOWN. IN THE MORNING, WE'LL GO SEE IF THEY CAN HELP US FIND THE OWNER.
AND WE NEED TO GO TO THE FABRIC STORE FOR THE STUFF TO MAKE OUR CHINESE NEW YEAR DRAGON.
OKAY, BUT DON'T PLAN ON GETTING UP TOO EARLY!
I'M GOING TO TELL SCARY STORIES THAT COULD KEEP YOU UP ALL NIGHT!
HEH
GR-GREAT?

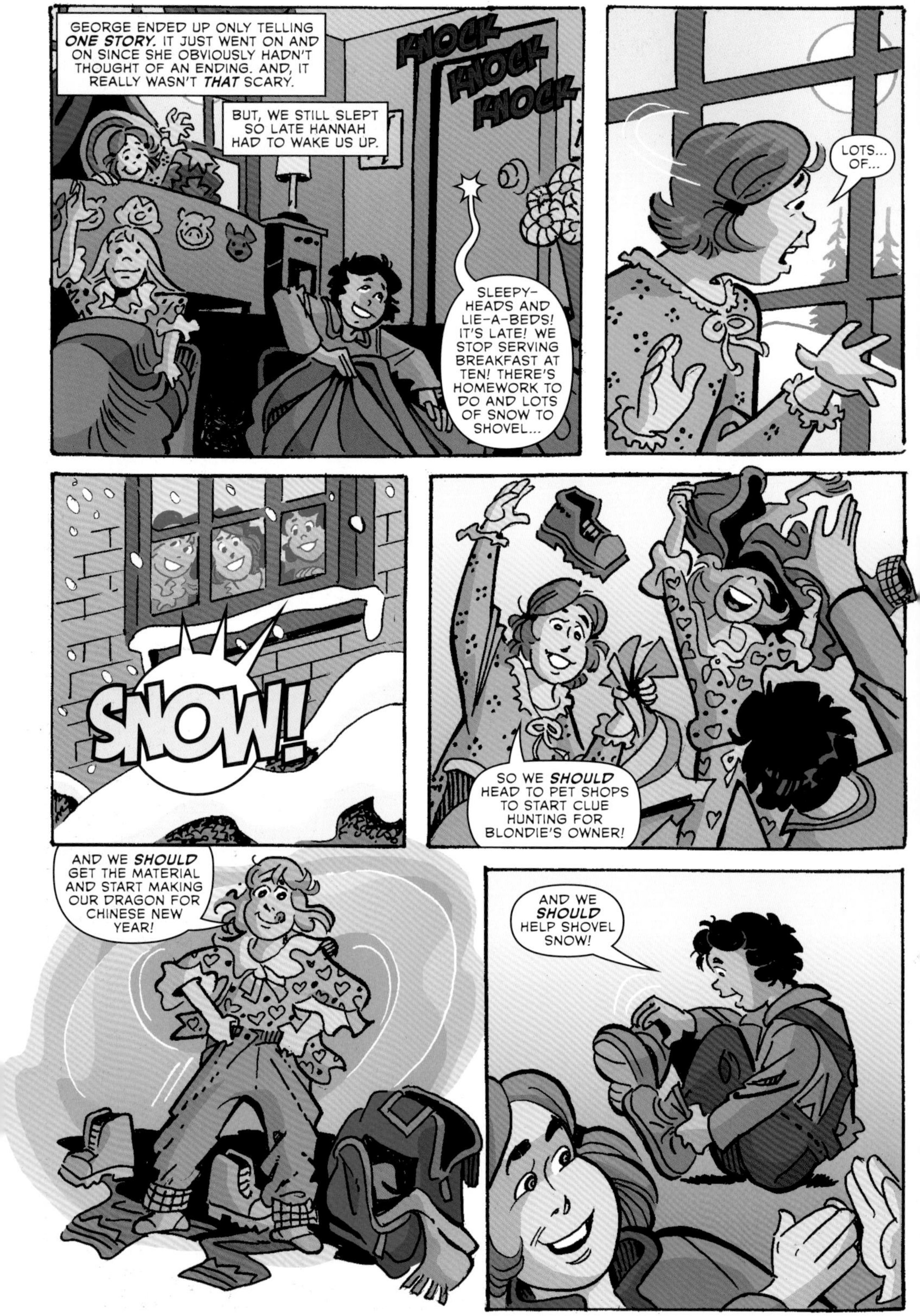
GEORGE ENDED UP ONLY TELLING ONE STORY. IT JUST WENT ON AND ON SINCE SHE OBVIOUSLY HADN'T THOUGHT OF AN ENDING. AND, IT REALLY WASN'T THAT SCARY.
KNOCK KNOCK KNOCK
BUT, WE STILL SLEPT SO LATE HANNAH HAD TO WAKE US UP.
SLEEPY-HEADS AND LIE-A-BEDS! IT'S LATE! WE STOP SERVING BREAKFAST AT TEN! THERE'S HOMEWORK TO DO AND LOTS OF SNOW TO SHOVEL...
LOTS... OF...
SNOW!
SO WE SHOULD HEAD TO PET SHOPS TO START CLUE HUNTING FOR BLONDIE'S OWNER!
AND WE SHOULD GET THE MATERIAL AND START MAKING OUR DRAGON FOR CHINESE NEW YEAR!
AND WE SHOULD HELP SHOVEL SNOW!

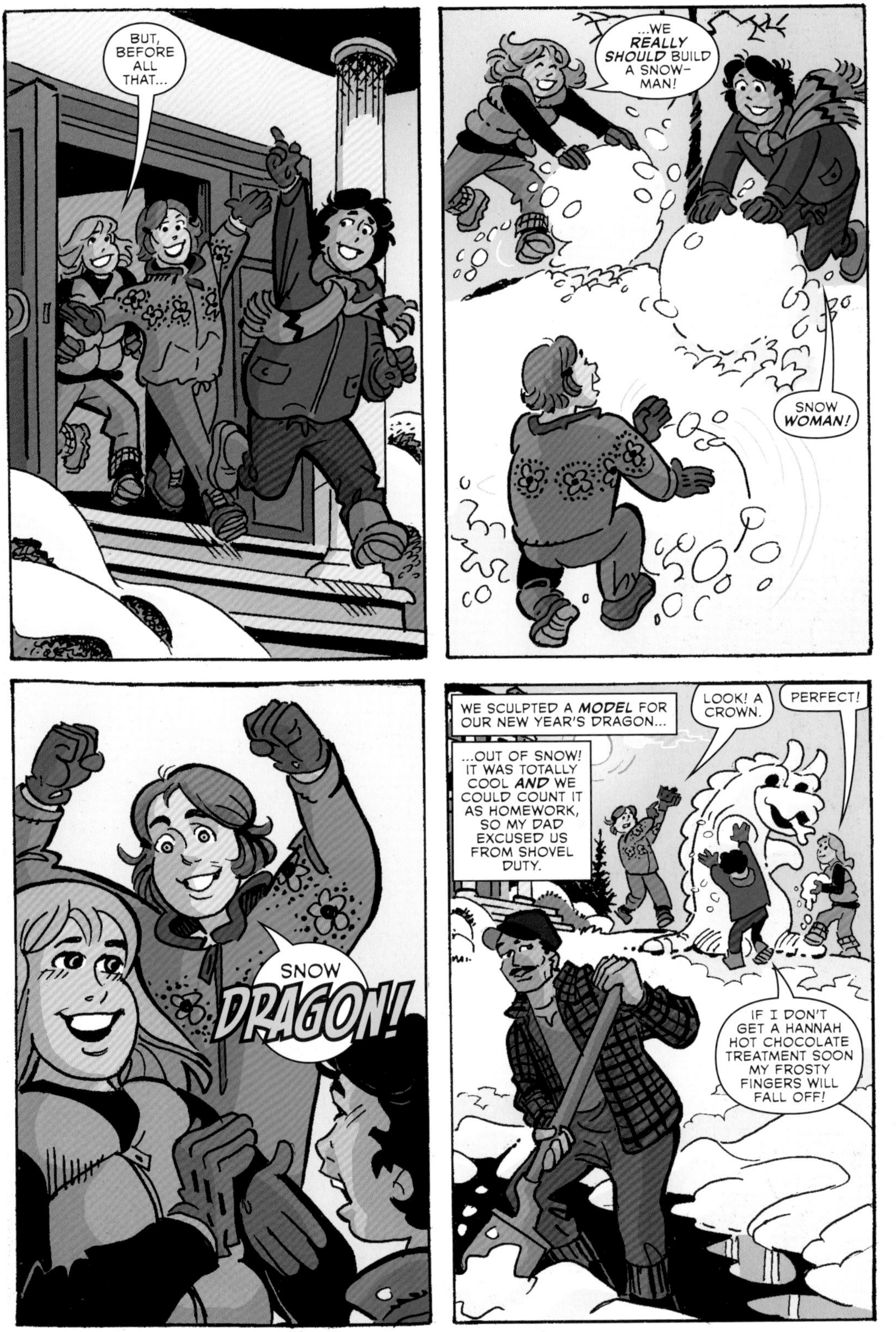
BUT, BEFORE ALL THAT...
...WE REALLY SHOULD BUILD A SNOW-MAN!
SNOW WOMAN!
SNOW DRAGON!
WE SCULPTED A MODEL FOR OUR NEW YEAR'S DRAGON...
...OUT OF SNOW! IT WAS TOTALLY COOL AND WE COULD COUNT IT AS HOMEWORK, SO MY DAD EXCUSED US FROM SHOVEL DUTY.
LOOK! A CROWN.
PERFECT!
IF I DON'T GET A HANNAH HOT CHOCOLATE TREATMENT SOON MY FROSTY FINGERS WILL FALL OFF!

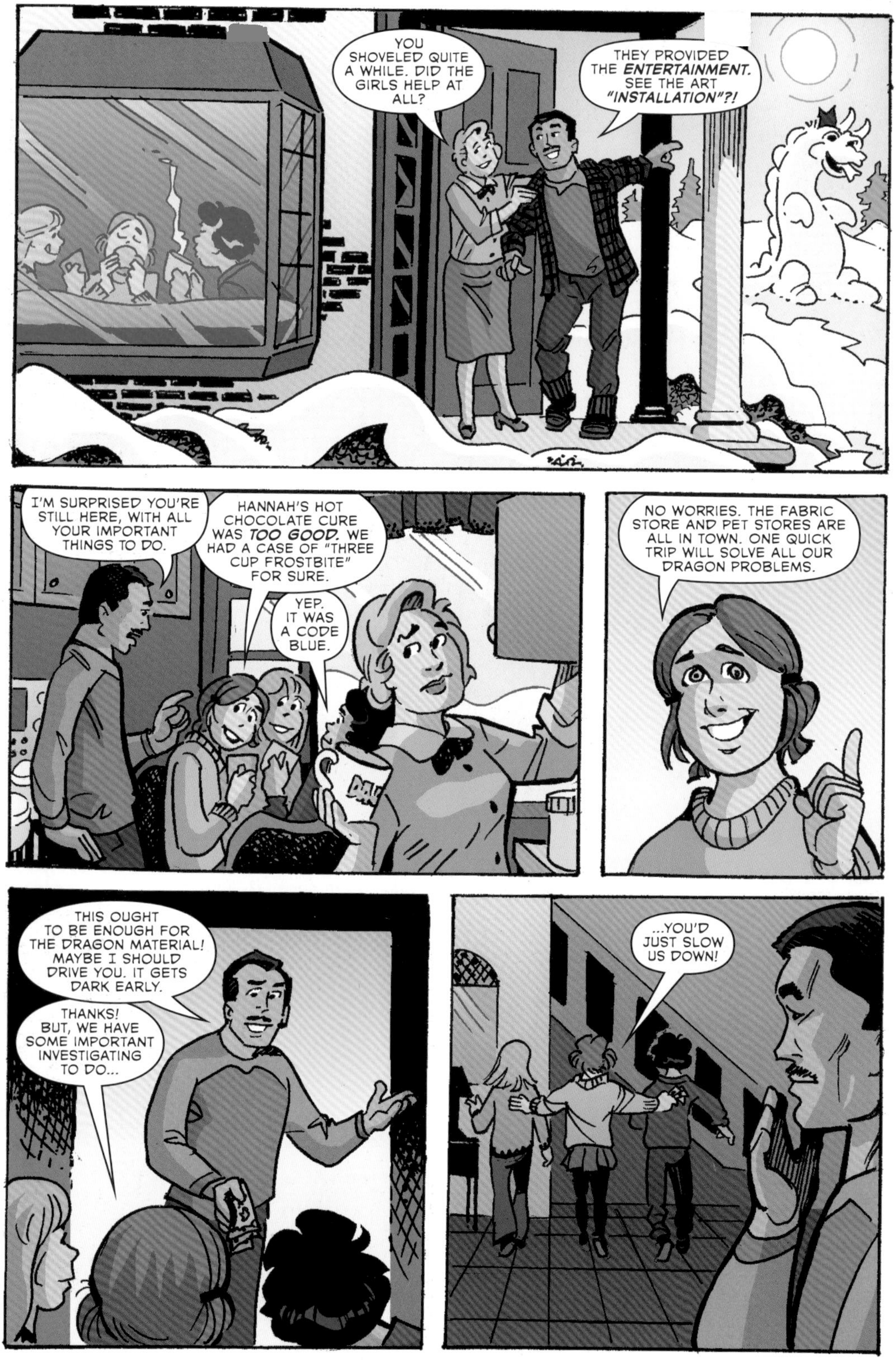
YOU SHOVELED QUITE A WHILE. DID THE GIRLS HELP AT ALL?
THEY PROVIDED THE ENTERTAINMENT. SEE THE ART "INSTALLATION"?!
I'M SURPRISED YOU'RE STILL HERE, WITH ALL YOUR IMPORTANT THINGS TO DO.
HANNAH'S HOT CHOCOLATE CURE WAS TOO GOOD. WE HAD A CASE OF "THREE CUP FROSTBITE" FOR SURE.
YEP. IT WAS A CODE BLUE.
NO WORRIES. THE FABRIC STORE AND PET STORES ARE ALL IN TOWN. ONE QUICK TRIP WILL SOLVE ALL OUR DRAGON PROBLEMS.
THIS OUGHT TO BE ENOUGH FOR THE DRAGON MATERIAL! MAYBE I SHOULD DRIVE YOU. IT GETS DARK EARLY.
THANKS! BUT, WE HAVE SOME IMPORTANT INVESTIGATING TO DO...
...YOU'D JUST SLOW US DOWN!

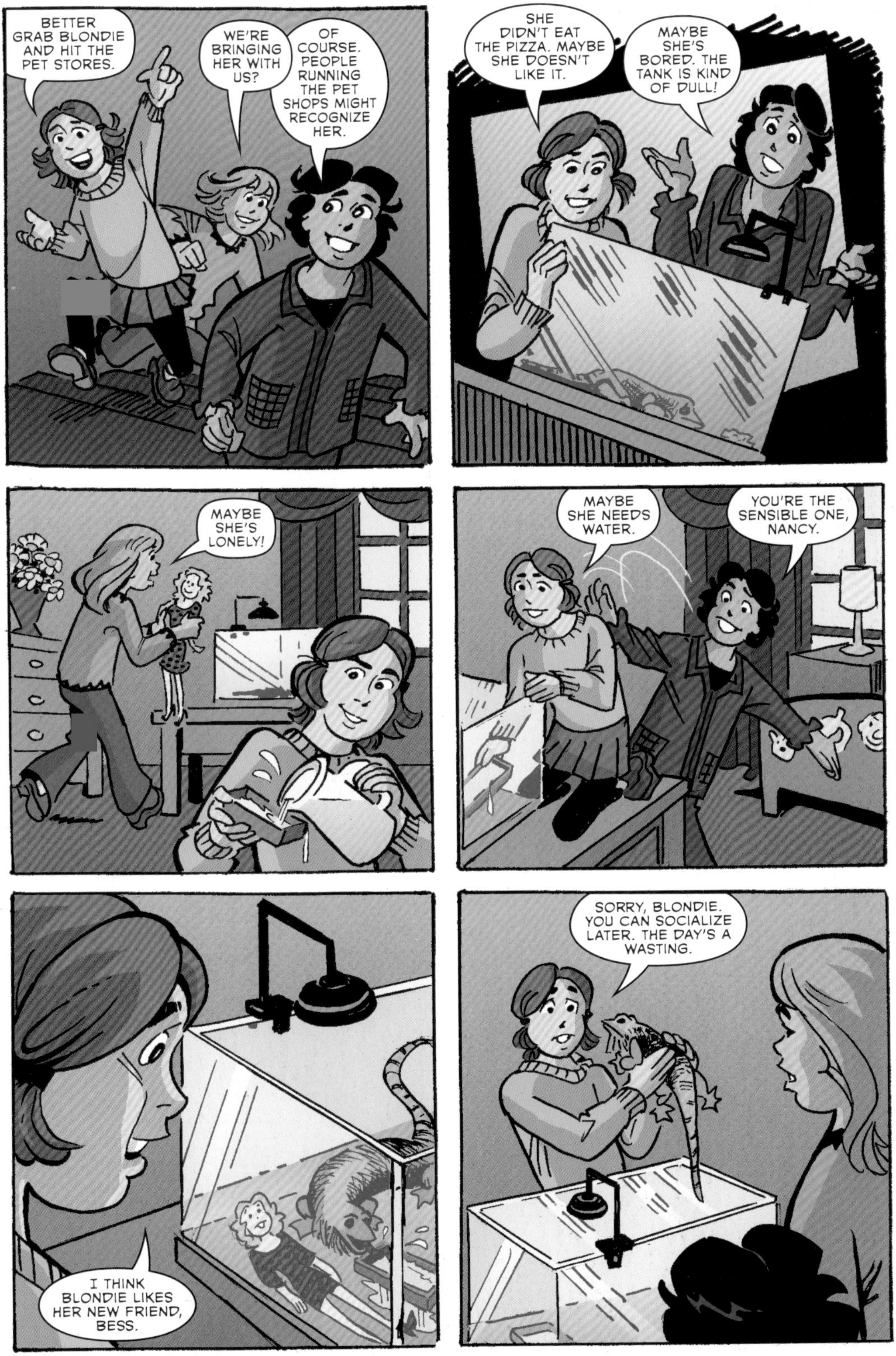
BETTER GRAB BLONDIE AND HIT THE PET STORES.
WE'RE BRINGING HER WITH US?
OF COURSE. PEOPLE RUNNING THE PET SHOPS MIGHT RECOGNIZE HER.
SHE DIDN'T EAT THE PIZZA. MAYBE SHE DOESN'T LIKE IT.
MAYBE SHE'S BORED. THE TANK IS KIND OF DULL!
MAYBE SHE'S LONELY!
MAYBE SHE NEEDS WATER.
YOU'RE THE SENSIBLE ONE, NANCY.
I THINK BLONDIE LIKES HER NEW FRIEND, BESS.
SORRY, BLONDIE. YOU CAN SOCIALIZE LATER. THE DAY'S A WASTING.

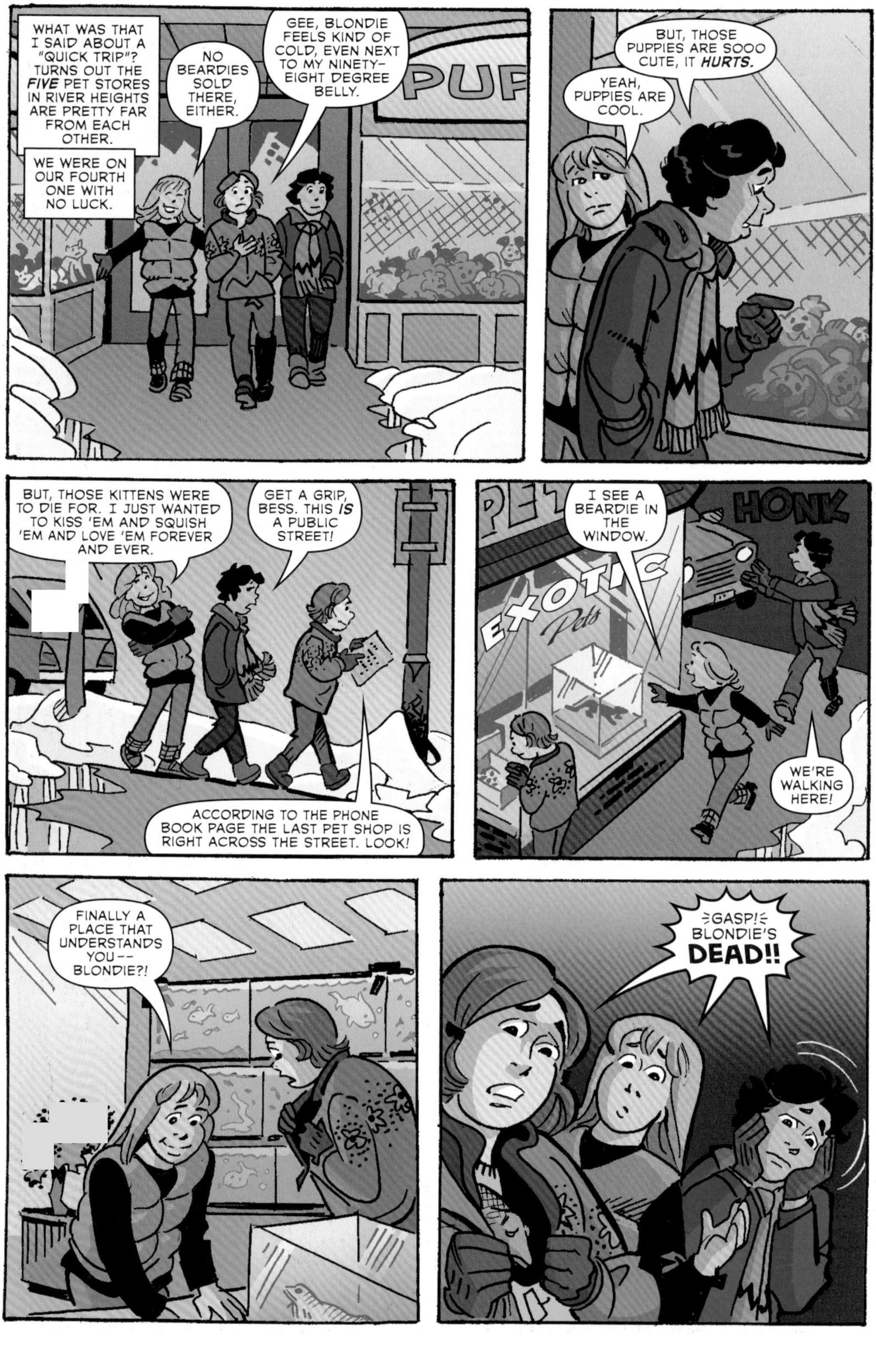
WHAT WAS THAT I SAID ABOUT A "QUICK TRIP"? TURNS OUT THE FIVE PET STORES IN RIVER HEIGHTS ARE PRETTY FAR FROM EACH OTHER.
WE WERE ON OUR FOURTH ONE WITH NO LUCK.
NO BEARDIES SOLD THERE, EITHER.
GEE, BLONDIE FEELS KIND OF COLD, EVEN NEXT TO MY NINETY-EIGHT DEGREE BELLY.
PUP
BUT, THOSE PUPPIES ARE SOOO CUTE, IT HURTS.
YEAH, PUPPIES ARE COOL.
BUT, THOSE KITTENS WERE TO DIE FOR. I JUST WANTED TO KISS 'EM AND SQUISH 'EM AND LOVE 'EM FOREVER AND EVER.
GET A GRIP, BESS. THIS IS A PUBLIC STREET!
ACCORDING TO THE PHONE BOOK PAGE THE LAST PET SHOP IS RIGHT ACROSS THE STREET. LOOK!
I SEE A BEARDIE IN THE WINDOW.
HONK
EXOTIC Pets
WE'RE WALKING HERE!
FINALLY A PLACE THAT UNDERSTANDS YOU-- BLONDIE?!
GASP! BLONDIE'S DEAD!!

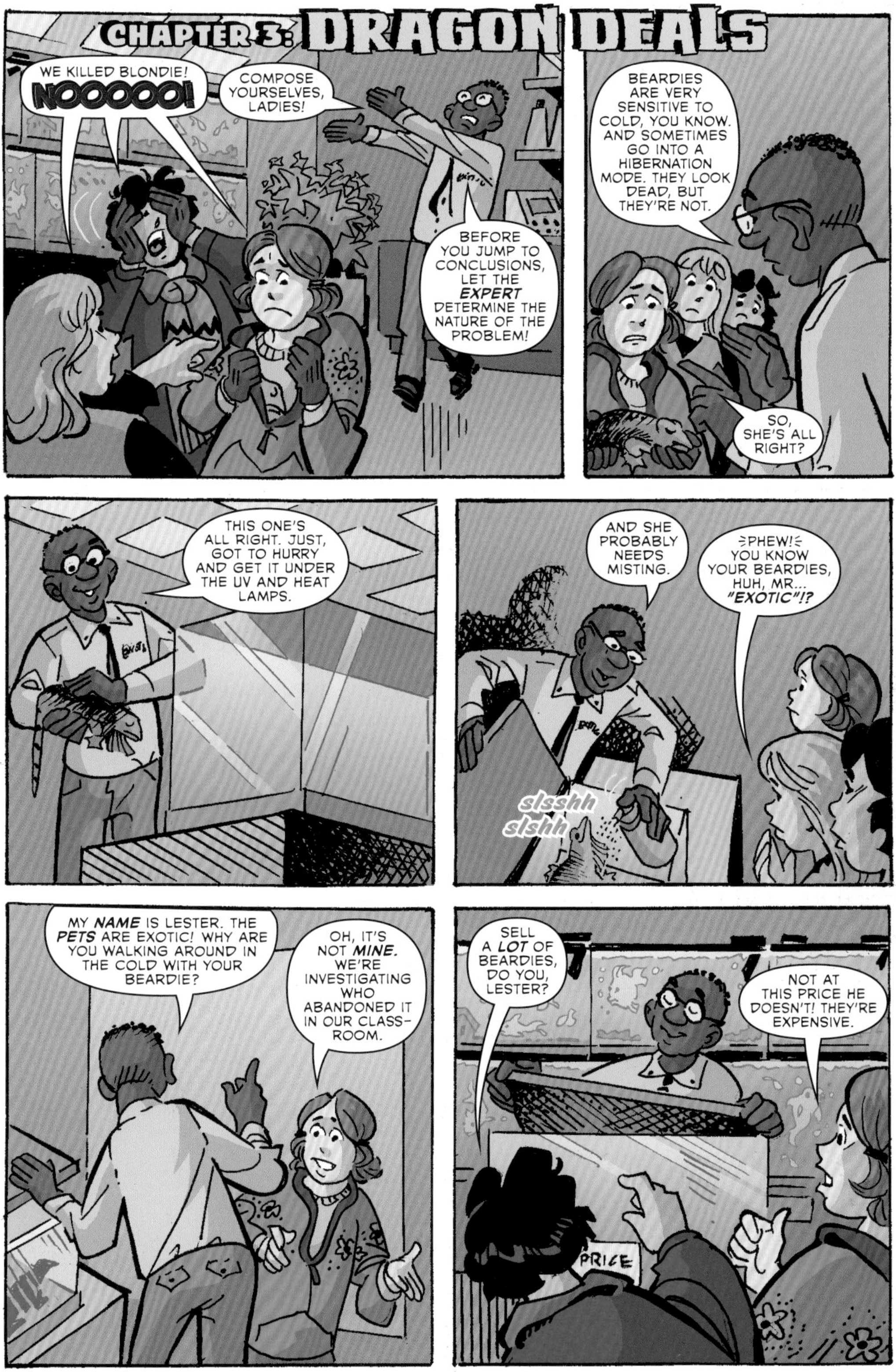
CHAPTER 3: DRAGON DEALS
WE KILLED BLONDIE!
NOOOOOO!
COMPOSE YOURSELVES, LADIES!
BEFORE YOU JUMP TO CONCLUSIONS, LET THE *EXPERT* DETERMINE THE NATURE OF THE PROBLEM!
BEARDIES ARE VERY SENSITIVE TO COLD, YOU KNOW. AND SOMETIMES GO INTO A HIBERNATION MODE. THEY LOOK DEAD, BUT THEY'RE NOT.
SO, SHE'S ALL RIGHT?
THIS ONE'S ALL RIGHT. JUST, GOT TO HURRY AND GET IT UNDER THE UV AND HEAT LAMPS.
AND SHE PROBABLY NEEDS MISTING.
PHEW! YOU KNOW YOUR BEARDIES, HUH, MR... *"EXOTIC"!?*
slsshh
slshh
MY *NAME* IS LESTER. THE *PETS* ARE EXOTIC! WHY ARE YOU WALKING AROUND IN THE COLD WITH YOUR BEARDIE?
OH, IT'S NOT *MINE.* WE'RE INVESTIGATING WHO ABANDONED IT IN OUR CLASS-ROOM.
SELL A *LOT* OF BEARDIES, DO YOU, LESTER?
NOT AT THIS PRICE HE DOESN'T! THEY'RE EXPENSIVE.
PRICE

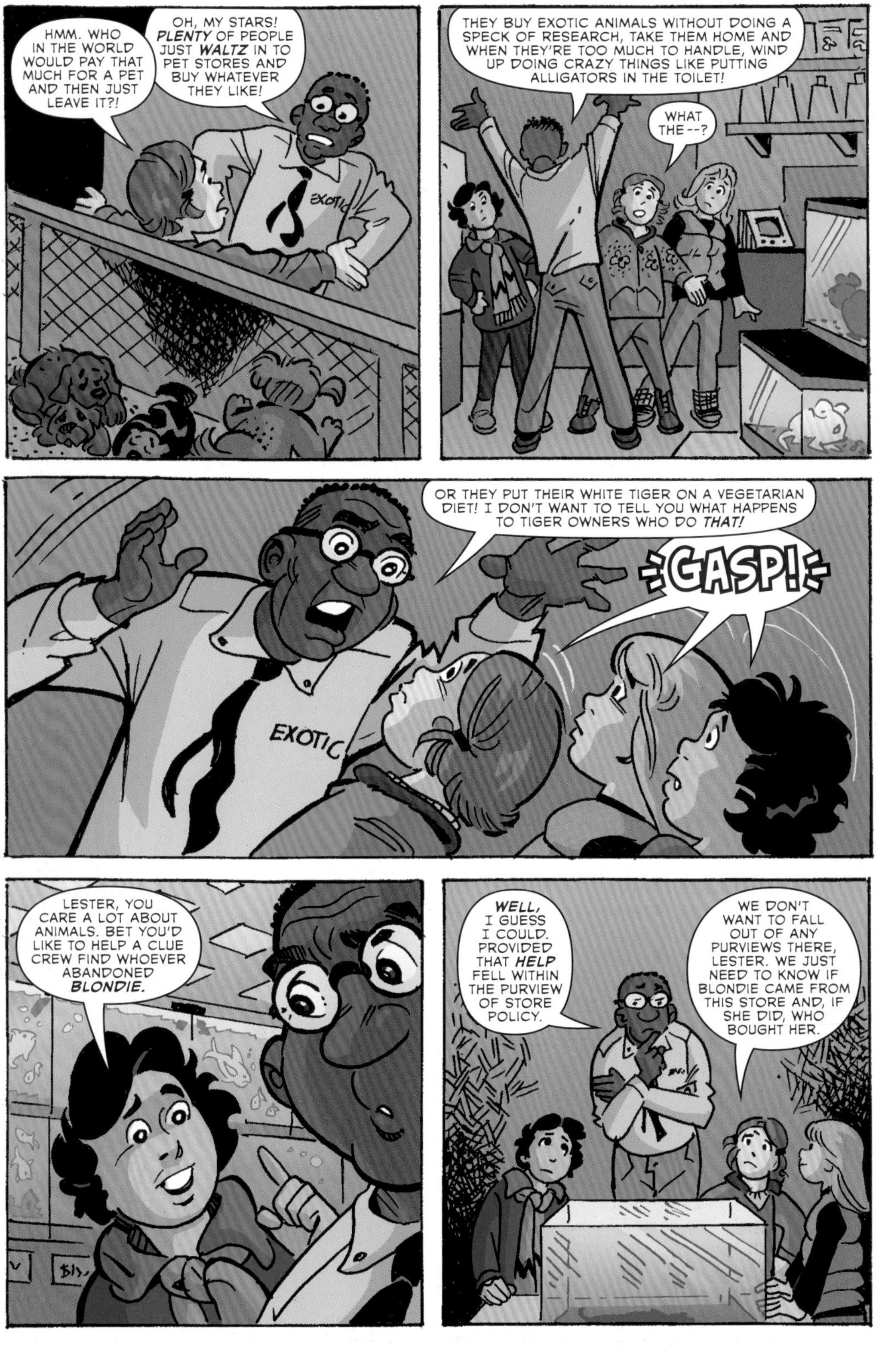
HMM. WHO IN THE WORLD WOULD PAY THAT MUCH FOR A PET AND THEN JUST LEAVE IT?!
OH, MY STARS! PLENTY OF PEOPLE JUST WALTZ IN TO PET STORES AND BUY WHATEVER THEY LIKE!
EXOTIC
THEY BUY EXOTIC ANIMALS WITHOUT DOING A SPECK OF RESEARCH, TAKE THEM HOME AND WHEN THEY'RE TOO MUCH TO HANDLE, WIND UP DOING CRAZY THINGS LIKE PUTTING ALLIGATORS IN THE TOILET!
WHAT THE--?
OR THEY PUT THEIR WHITE TIGER ON A VEGETARIAN DIET! I DON'T WANT TO TELL YOU WHAT HAPPENS TO TIGER OWNERS WHO DO THAT!
GASP!
EXOTIC
LESTER, YOU CARE A LOT ABOUT ANIMALS. BET YOU'D LIKE TO HELP A CLUE CREW FIND WHOEVER ABANDONED BLONDIE.
WELL, I GUESS I COULD. PROVIDED THAT HELP FELL WITHIN THE PURVIEW OF STORE POLICY.
WE DON'T WANT TO FALL OUT OF ANY PURVIEWS THERE, LESTER. WE JUST NEED TO KNOW IF BLONDIE CAME FROM THIS STORE AND, IF SHE DID, WHO BOUGHT HER.

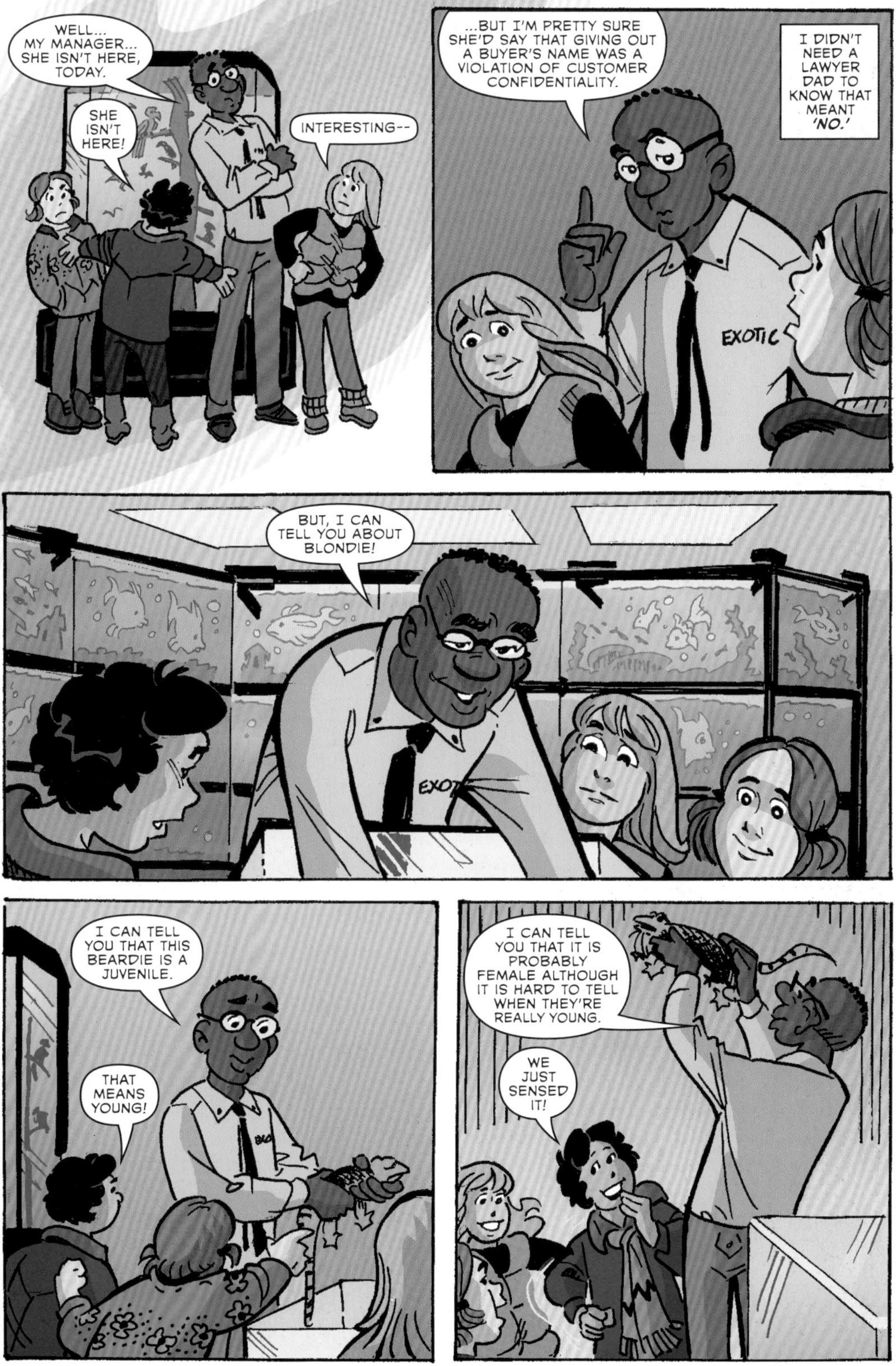
WELL... MY MANAGER... SHE ISN'T HERE, TODAY.
SHE ISN'T HERE!
INTERESTING--
...BUT I'M PRETTY SURE SHE'D SAY THAT GIVING OUT A BUYER'S NAME WAS A VIOLATION OF CUSTOMER CONFIDENTIALITY.
I DIDN'T NEED A LAWYER DAD TO KNOW THAT MEANT *'NO.'*
EXOTIC
BUT, I CAN TELL YOU ABOUT BLONDIE!
EXO
I CAN TELL YOU THAT THIS BEARDIE IS A JUVENILE.
THAT MEANS YOUNG!
I CAN TELL YOU THAT IT IS PROBABLY FEMALE ALTHOUGH IT IS HARD TO TELL WHEN THEY'RE REALLY YOUNG.
WE JUST SENSED IT!

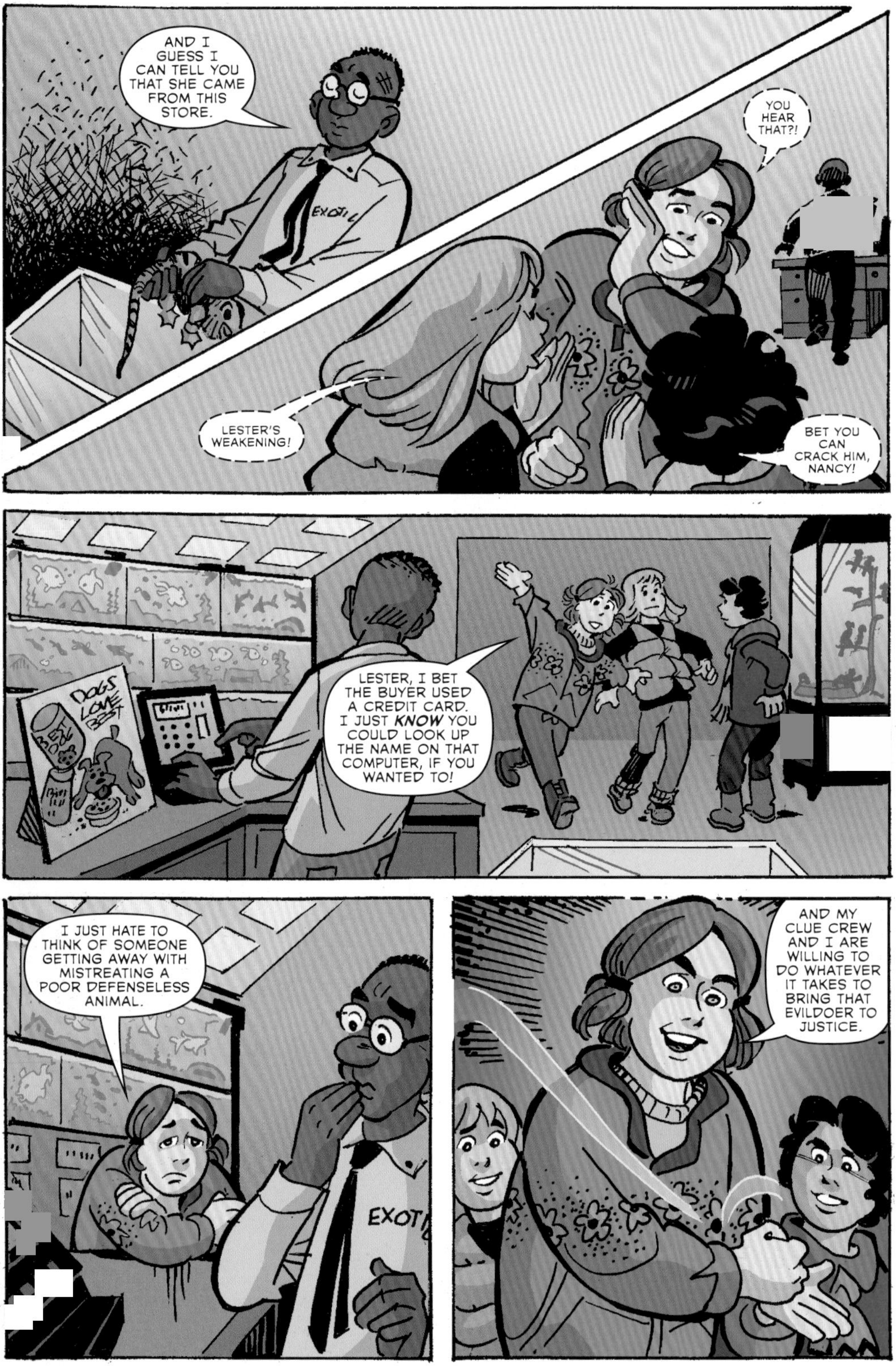
AND I GUESS I CAN TELL YOU THAT SHE CAME FROM THIS STORE.
YOU HEAR THAT?!
LESTER'S WEAKENING!
BET YOU CAN CRACK HIM, NANCY!
LESTER, I BET THE BUYER USED A CREDIT CARD. I JUST *KNOW* YOU COULD LOOK UP THE NAME ON THAT COMPUTER, IF YOU WANTED TO!
I JUST HATE TO THINK OF SOMEONE GETTING AWAY WITH MISTREATING A POOR DEFENSELESS ANIMAL.
AND MY CLUE CREW AND I ARE WILLING TO DO WHATEVER IT TAKES TO BRING THAT EVILDOER TO JUSTICE.

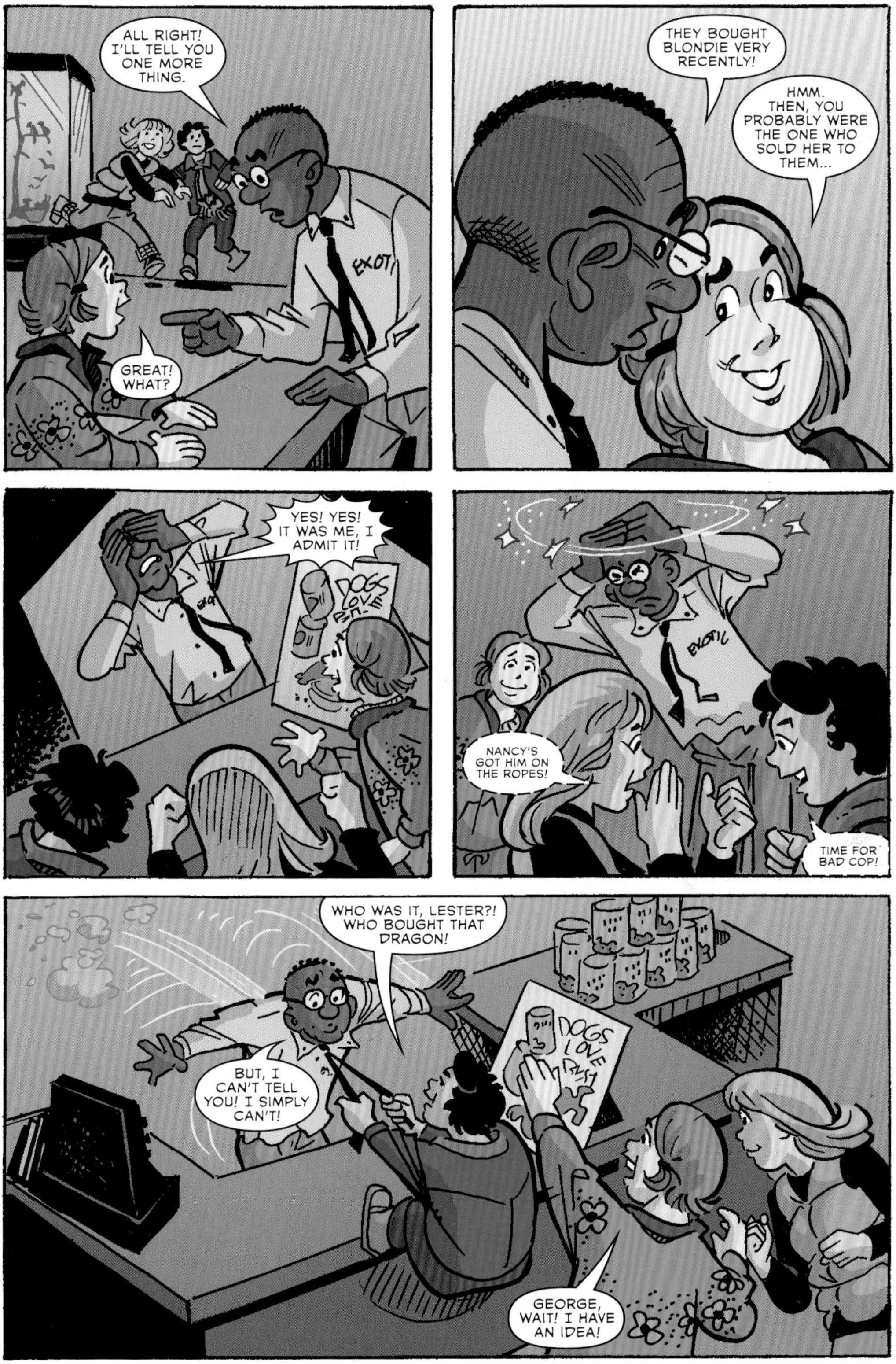
ALL RIGHT! I'LL TELL YOU ONE MORE THING.
GREAT! WHAT?
THEY BOUGHT BLONDIE VERY RECENTLY!
HMM. THEN, YOU PROBABLY WERE THE ONE WHO SOLD HER TO THEM...
YES! YES! IT WAS ME, I ADMIT IT!
NANCY'S GOT HIM ON THE ROPES!
TIME FOR BAD COP!
WHO WAS IT, LESTER?! WHO BOUGHT THAT DRAGON!
BUT, I CAN'T TELL YOU! I SIMPLY CAN'T!
GEORGE, WAIT! I HAVE AN IDEA!

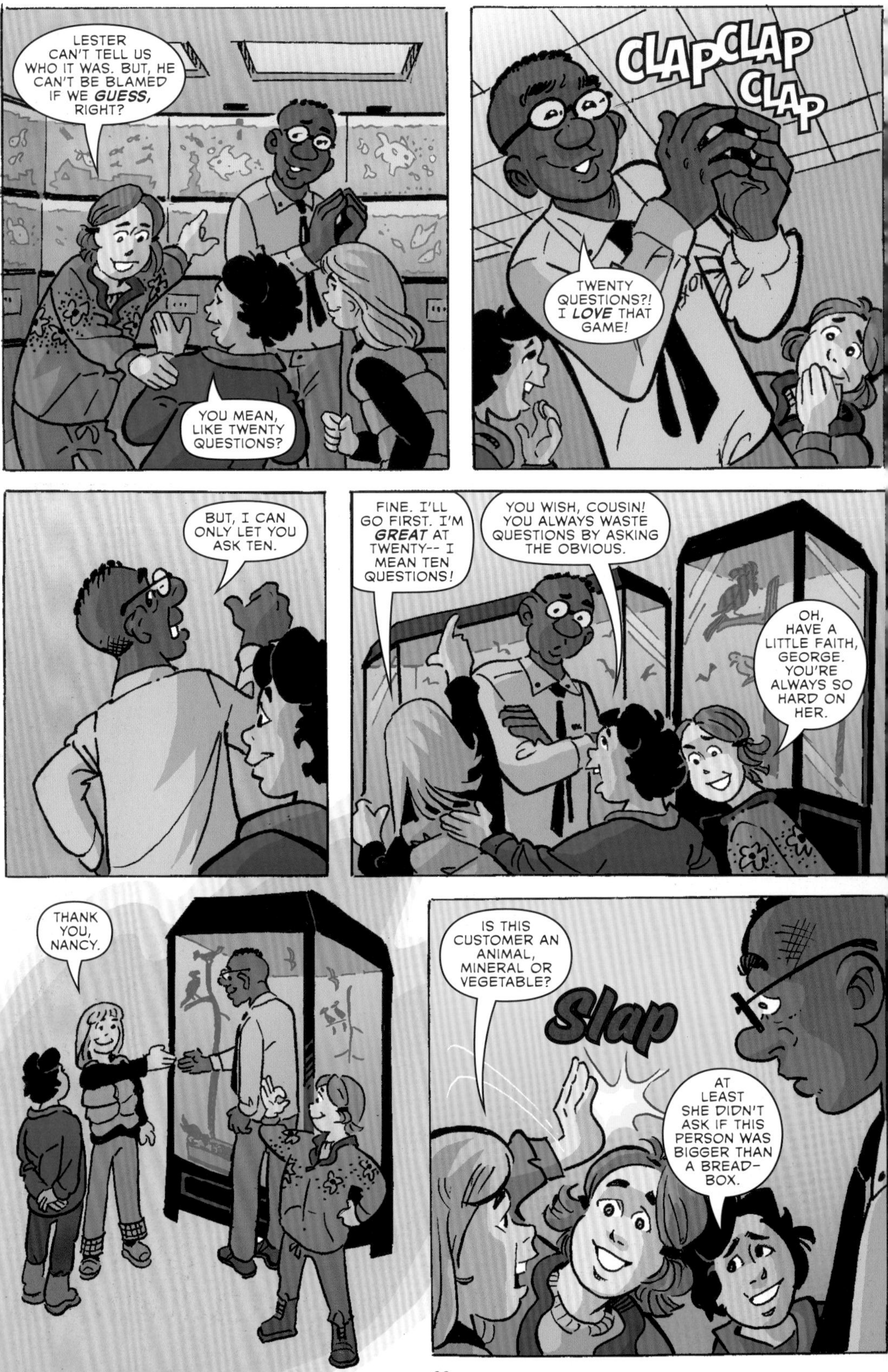

LESTER CAN'T TELL US WHO IT WAS. BUT, HE CAN'T BE BLAMED IF WE GUESS, RIGHT?
YOU MEAN, LIKE TWENTY QUESTIONS?
CLAPCLAP CLAP
TWENTY QUESTIONS?! I LOVE THAT GAME!
BUT, I CAN ONLY LET YOU ASK TEN.
FINE. I'LL GO FIRST. I'M GREAT AT TWENTY-- I MEAN TEN QUESTIONS!
YOU WISH, COUSIN! YOU ALWAYS WASTE QUESTIONS BY ASKING THE OBVIOUS.
OH, HAVE A LITTLE FAITH, GEORGE. YOU'RE ALWAYS SO HARD ON HER.
THANK YOU, NANCY.
IS THIS CUSTOMER AN ANIMAL, MINERAL OR VEGETABLE?
Slap
AT LEAST SHE DIDN'T ASK IF THIS PERSON WAS BIGGER THAN A BREAD-BOX.

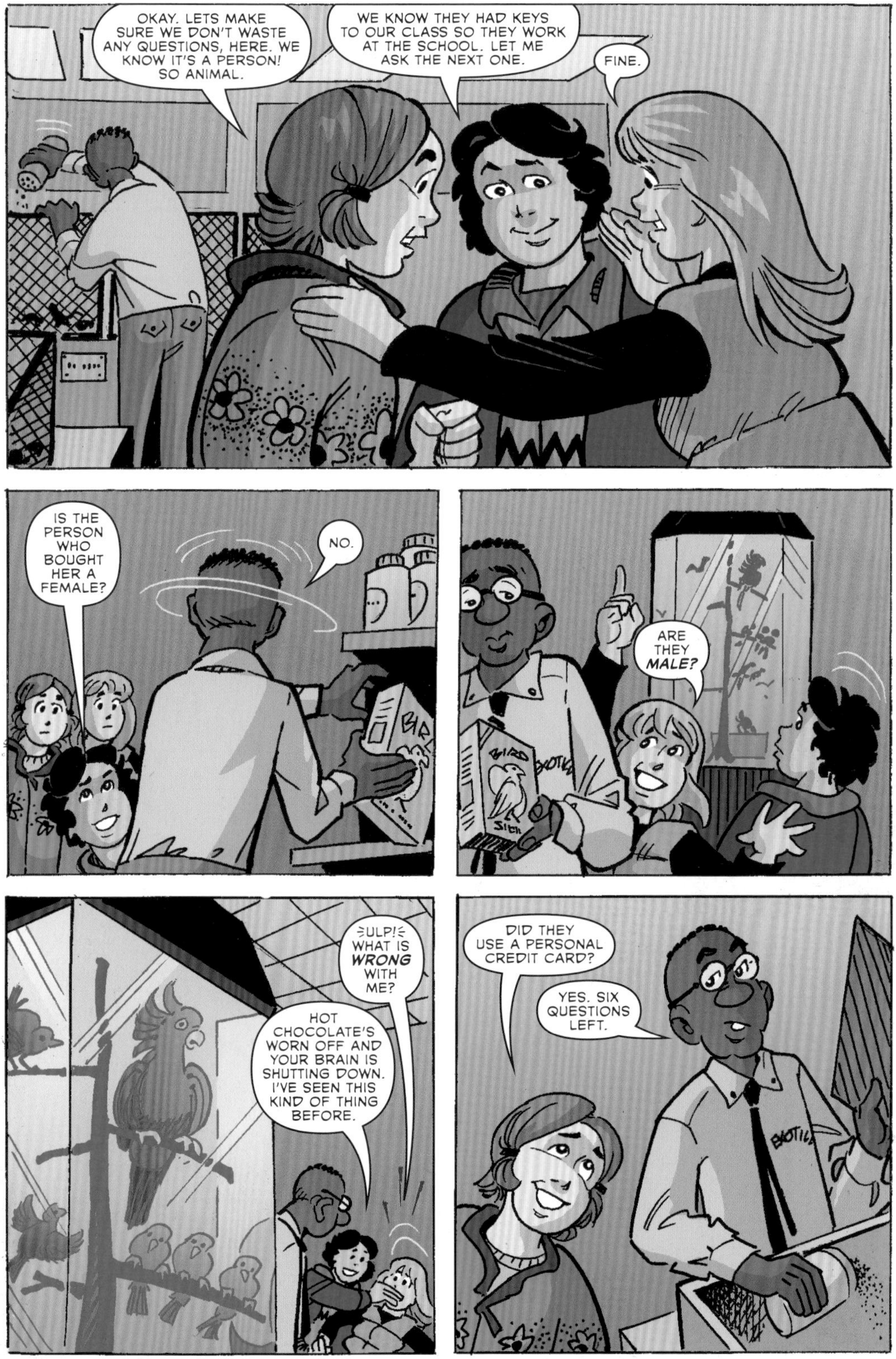
OKAY. LETS MAKE SURE WE DON'T WASTE ANY QUESTIONS, HERE. WE KNOW IT'S A PERSON! SO ANIMAL.
WE KNOW THEY HAD KEYS TO OUR CLASS SO THEY WORK AT THE SCHOOL. LET ME ASK THE NEXT ONE.
FINE.
IS THE PERSON WHO BOUGHT HER A FEMALE?
NO.
ARE THEY *MALE?*
ULP! WHAT IS *WRONG* WITH ME?
HOT CHOCOLATE'S WORN OFF AND YOUR BRAIN IS SHUTTING DOWN. I'VE SEEN THIS KIND OF THING BEFORE.
DID THEY USE A PERSONAL CREDIT CARD?
YES. SIX QUESTIONS LEFT.

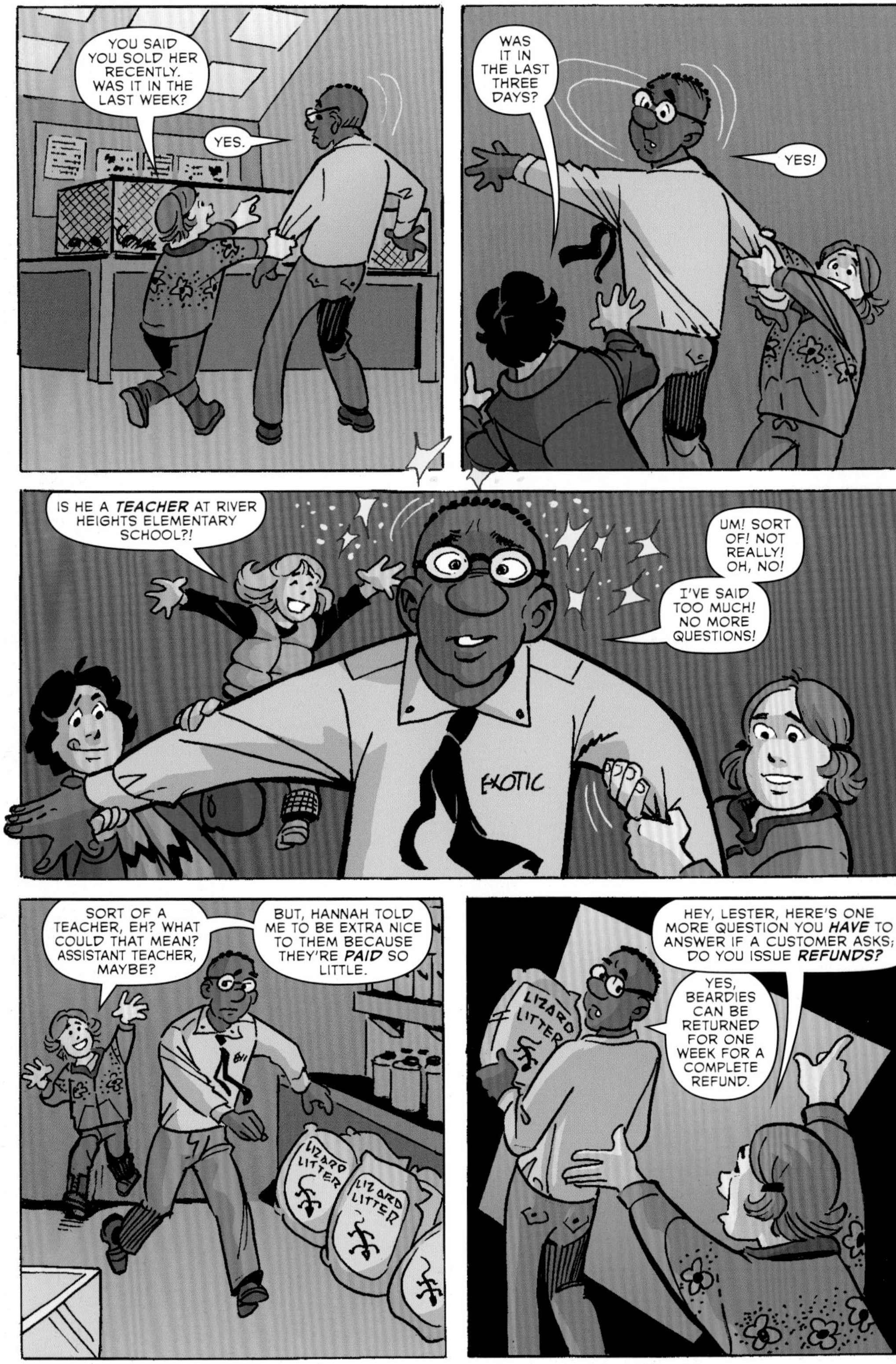
YOU SAID YOU SOLD HER RECENTLY. WAS IT IN THE LAST WEEK?
YES.
WAS IT IN THE LAST THREE DAYS?
YES!
IS HE A **TEACHER** AT RIVER HEIGHTS ELEMENTARY SCHOOL?!
UM! SORT OF! NOT REALLY! OH, NO!
I'VE SAID TOO MUCH! NO MORE QUESTIONS!
EXOTIC
SORT OF A TEACHER, EH? WHAT COULD THAT MEAN? ASSISTANT TEACHER, MAYBE?
BUT, HANNAH TOLD ME TO BE EXTRA NICE TO THEM BECAUSE THEY'RE **PAID** SO LITTLE.
LIZARD LITTER
LIZARD LITTER
HEY, LESTER, HERE'S ONE MORE QUESTION YOU **HAVE** TO ANSWER IF A CUSTOMER ASKS; DO YOU ISSUE **REFUNDS?**
YES, BEARDIES CAN BE RETURNED FOR ONE WEEK FOR A COMPLETE REFUND.
LIZARD LITTER

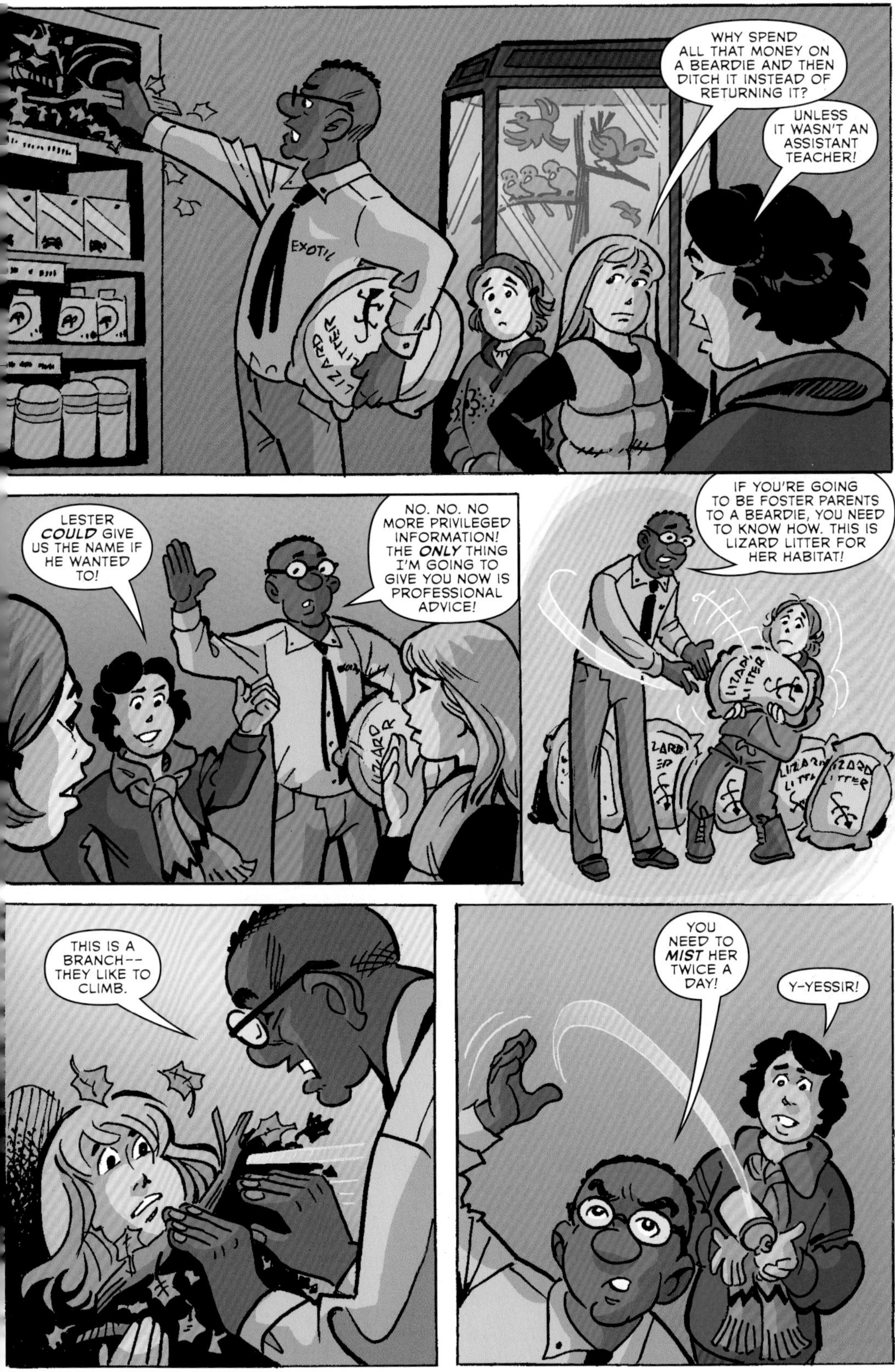
WHY SPEND ALL THAT MONEY ON A BEARDIE AND THEN DITCH IT INSTEAD OF RETURNING IT?
UNLESS IT WASN'T AN ASSISTANT TEACHER!
EXOTIC
LIZARD LITTER
LESTER COULD GIVE US THE NAME IF HE WANTED TO!
NO. NO. NO MORE PRIVILEGED INFORMATION! THE ONLY THING I'M GOING TO GIVE YOU NOW IS PROFESSIONAL ADVICE!
IF YOU'RE GOING TO BE FOSTER PARENTS TO A BEARDIE, YOU NEED TO KNOW HOW. THIS IS LIZARD LITTER FOR HER HABITAT!
LIZARD LITTER
THIS IS A BRANCH-- THEY LIKE TO CLIMB.
YOU NEED TO MIST HER TWICE A DAY!
Y-YESSIR!

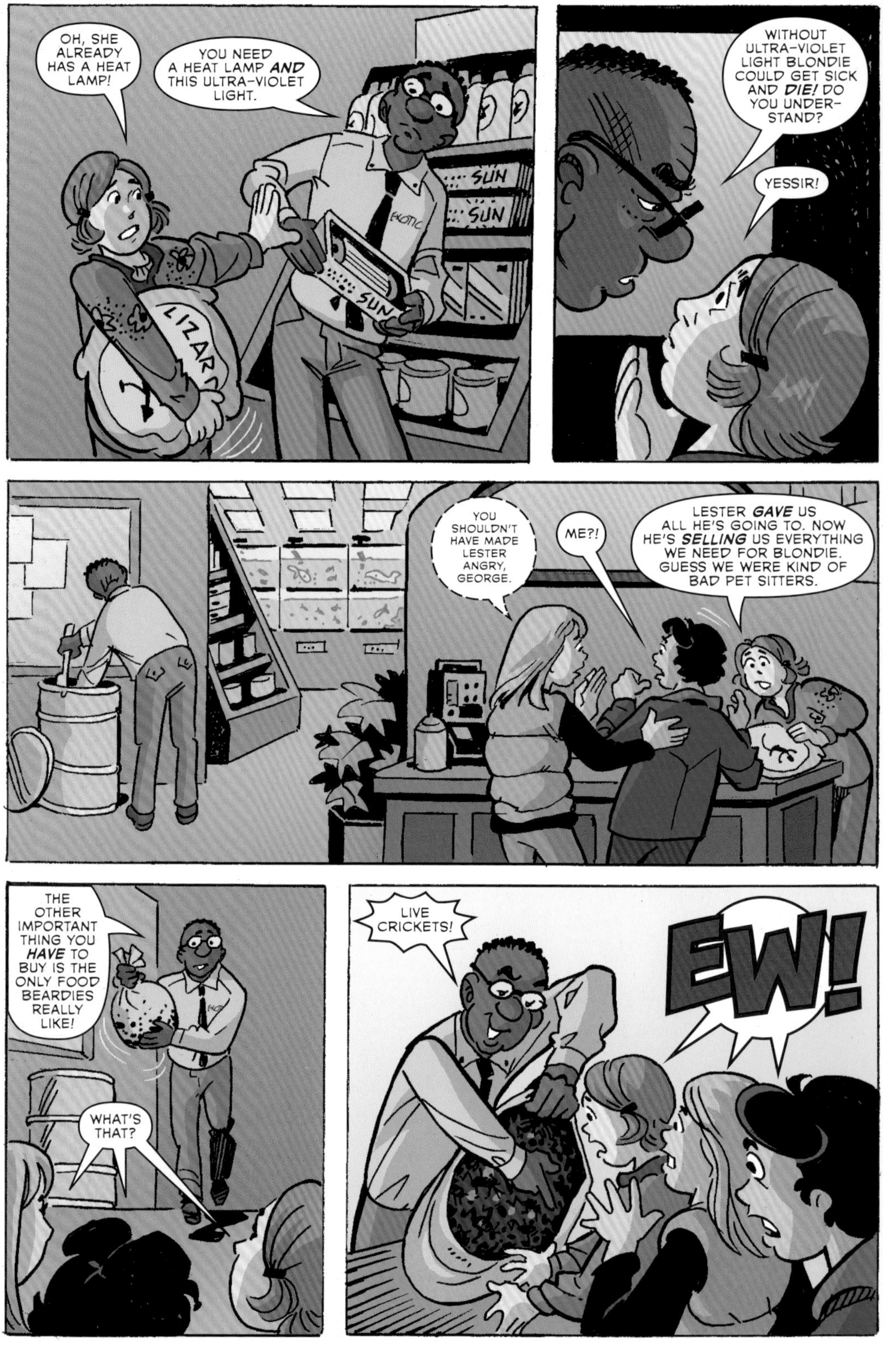
OH, SHE ALREADY HAS A HEAT LAMP!
YOU NEED A HEAT LAMP AND THIS ULTRA-VIOLET LIGHT.
SUN
SUN
EXOTIC
SUN
LIZARD
WITHOUT ULTRA-VIOLET LIGHT BLONDIE COULD GET SICK AND DIE! DO YOU UNDER-STAND?
YESSIR!
YOU SHOULDN'T HAVE MADE LESTER ANGRY, GEORGE.
ME?!
LESTER GAVE US ALL HE'S GOING TO. NOW HE'S SELLING US EVERYTHING WE NEED FOR BLONDIE. GUESS WE WERE KIND OF BAD PET SITTERS.
THE OTHER IMPORTANT THING YOU HAVE TO BUY IS THE ONLY FOOD BEARDIES REALLY LIKE!
WHAT'S THAT?
LIVE CRICKETS!
EW!

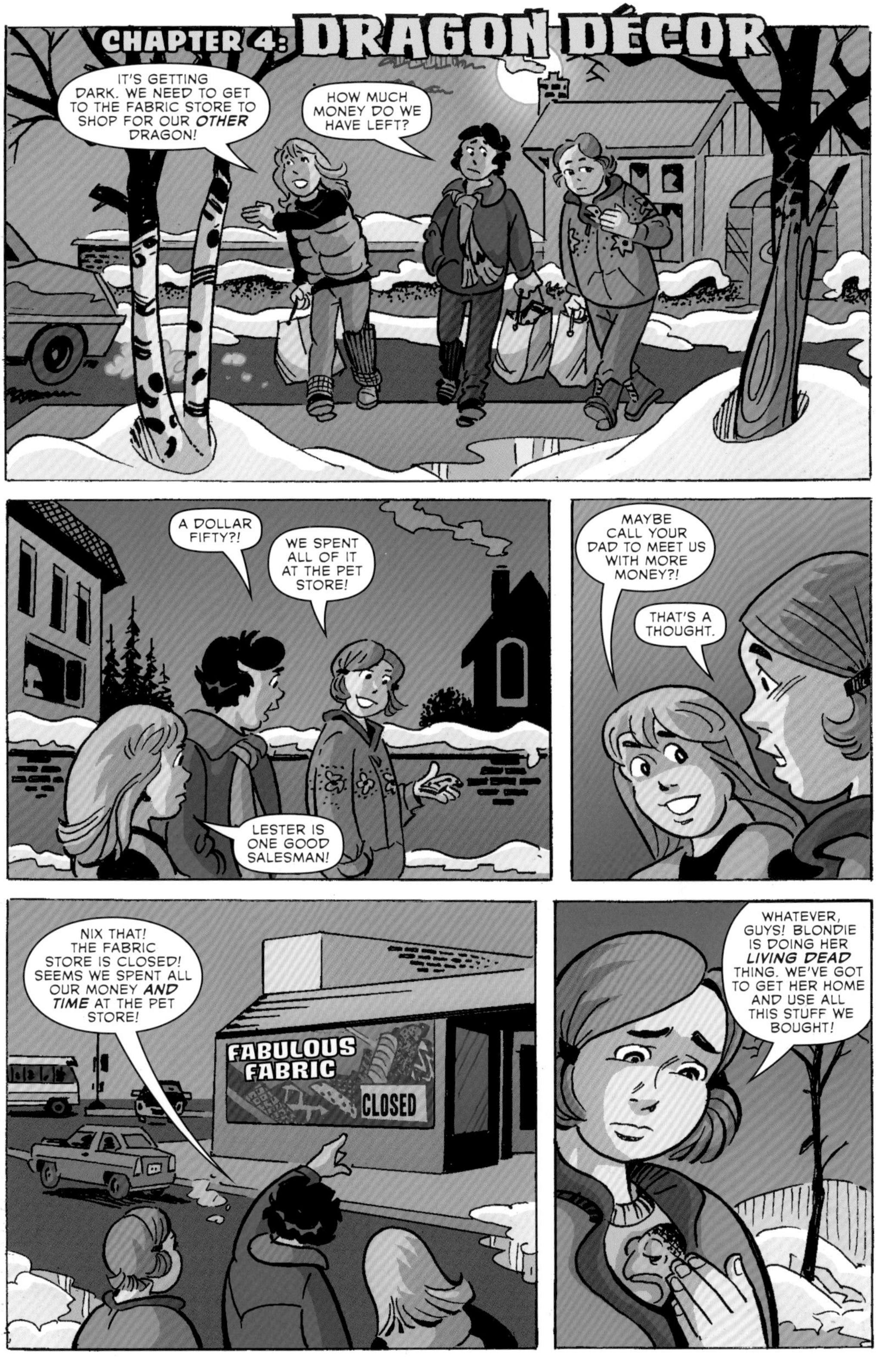
CHAPTER 4: DRAGON DÉCOR
IT'S GETTING DARK. WE NEED TO GET TO THE FABRIC STORE TO SHOP FOR OUR *OTHER* DRAGON!
HOW MUCH MONEY DO WE HAVE LEFT?
A DOLLAR FIFTY?!
WE SPENT ALL OF IT AT THE PET STORE!
LESTER IS ONE GOOD SALESMAN!
MAYBE CALL YOUR DAD TO MEET US WITH MORE MONEY?!
THAT'S A THOUGHT.
NIX THAT! THE FABRIC STORE IS CLOSED! SEEMS WE SPENT ALL OUR MONEY *AND TIME* AT THE PET STORE!
FABULOUS FABRIC
CLOSED
WHATEVER, GUYS! BLONDIE IS DOING HER *LIVING DEAD* THING. WE'VE GOT TO GET HER HOME AND USE ALL THIS STUFF WE BOUGHT!

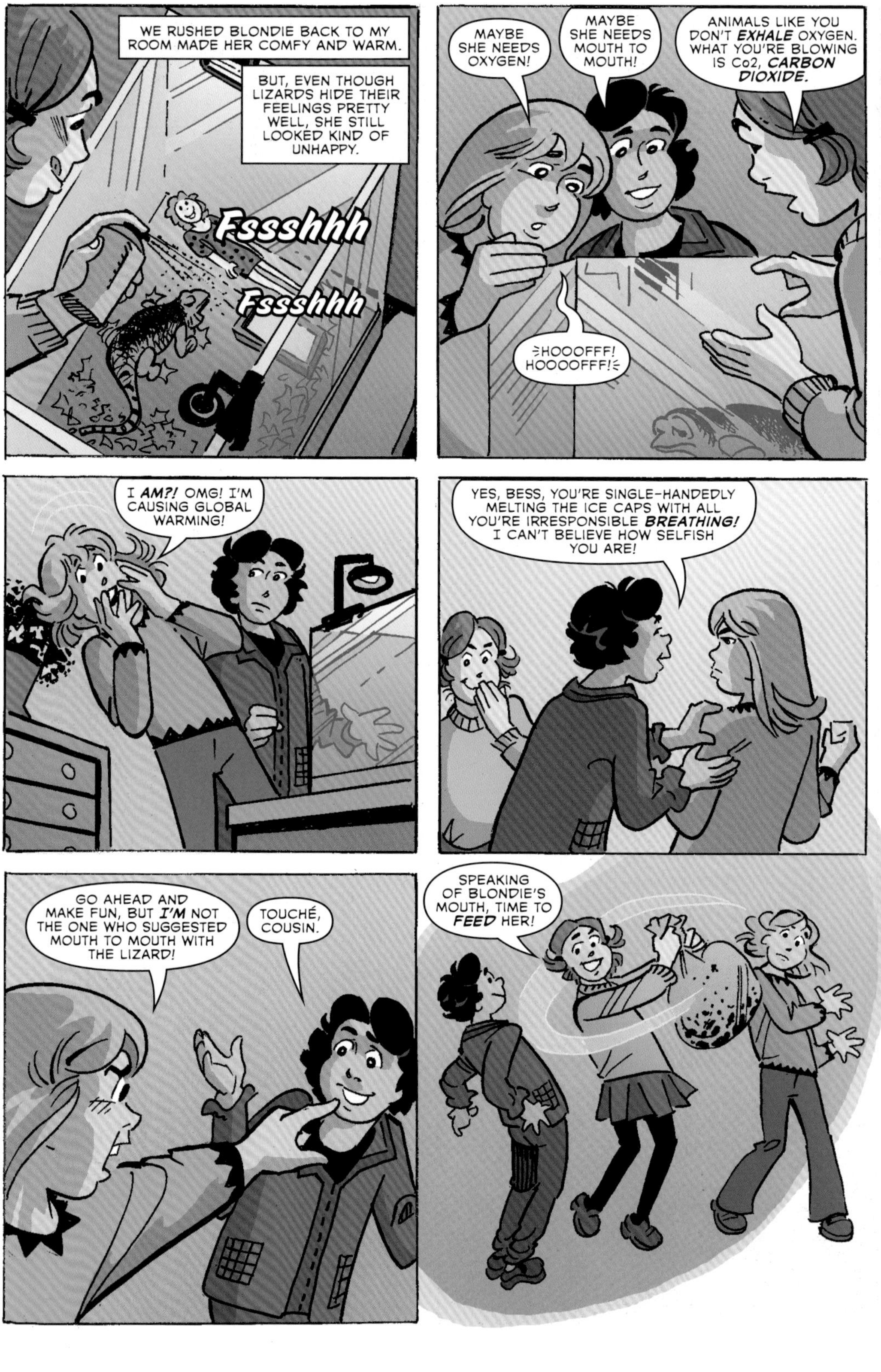
WE RUSHED BLONDIE BACK TO MY ROOM MADE HER COMFY AND WARM.
BUT, EVEN THOUGH LIZARDS HIDE THEIR FEELINGS PRETTY WELL, SHE STILL LOOKED KIND OF UNHAPPY.
Fssshhh
Fssshhh
MAYBE SHE NEEDS OXYGEN!
MAYBE SHE NEEDS MOUTH TO MOUTH!
ANIMALS LIKE YOU DON'T EXHALE OXYGEN. WHAT YOU'RE BLOWING IS Co2, CARBON DIOXIDE.
HOOOFFF! HOOOOFFF!
I AM?! OMG! I'M CAUSING GLOBAL WARMING!
YES, BESS, YOU'RE SINGLE-HANDEDLY MELTING THE ICE CAPS WITH ALL YOU'RE IRRESPONSIBLE BREATHING! I CAN'T BELIEVE HOW SELFISH YOU ARE!
GO AHEAD AND MAKE FUN, BUT I'M NOT THE ONE WHO SUGGESTED MOUTH TO MOUTH WITH THE LIZARD!
TOUCHÉ, COUSIN.
SPEAKING OF BLONDIE'S MOUTH, TIME TO FEED HER!

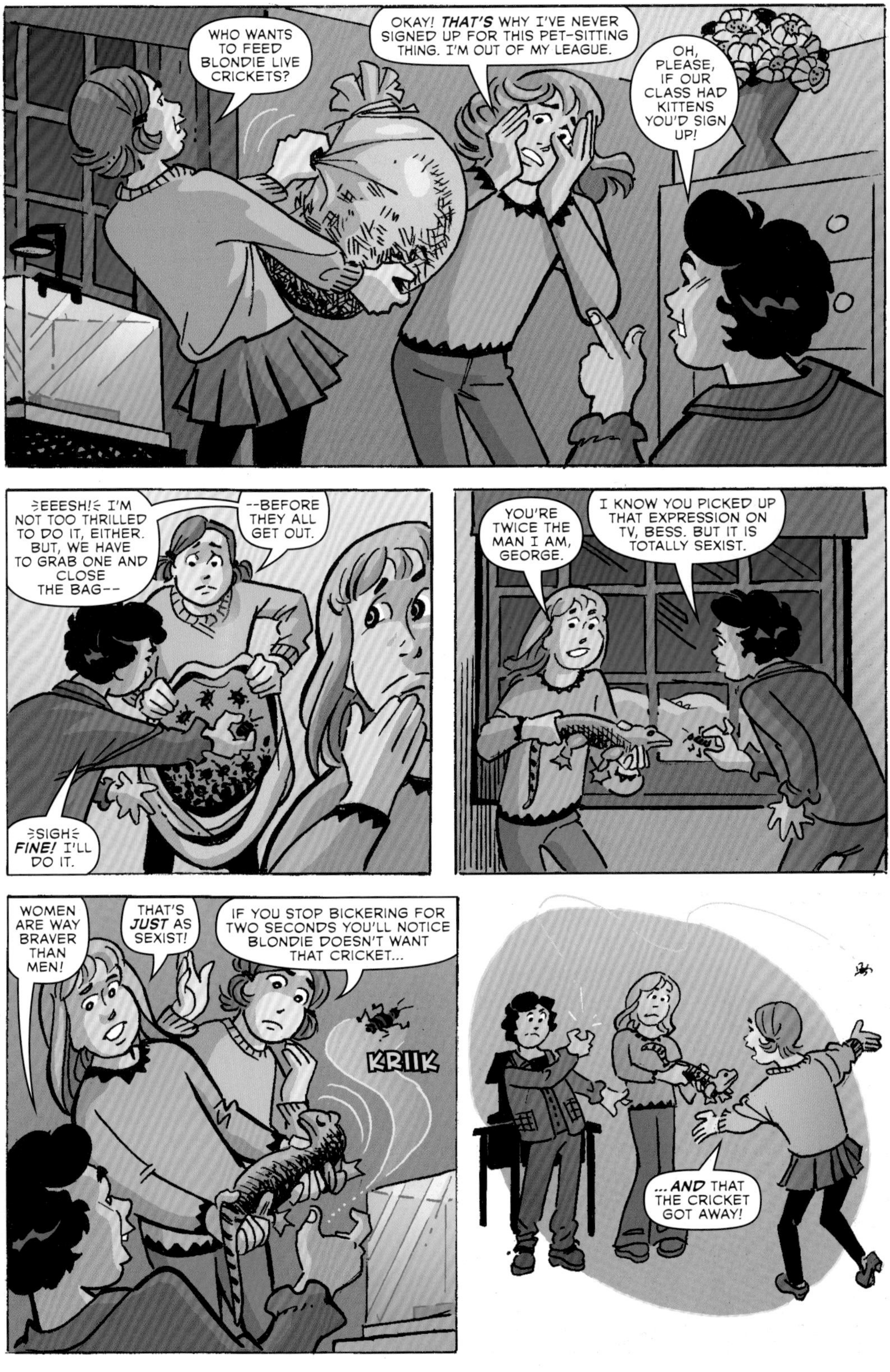

WHO WANTS TO FEED BLONDIE LIVE CRICKETS?
OKAY! THAT'S WHY I'VE NEVER SIGNED UP FOR THIS PET-SITTING THING. I'M OUT OF MY LEAGUE.
OH, PLEASE, IF OUR CLASS HAD KITTENS YOU'D SIGN UP!
⋛EEESH!⋚ I'M NOT TOO THRILLED TO DO IT, EITHER. BUT, WE HAVE TO GRAB ONE AND CLOSE THE BAG--
--BEFORE THEY ALL GET OUT.
⋛SIGH⋚ FINE! I'LL DO IT.
YOU'RE TWICE THE MAN I AM, GEORGE.
I KNOW YOU PICKED UP THAT EXPRESSION ON TV, BESS. BUT IT IS TOTALLY SEXIST.
WOMEN ARE WAY BRAVER THAN MEN!
THAT'S JUST AS SEXIST!
IF YOU STOP BICKERING FOR TWO SECONDS YOU'LL NOTICE BLONDIE DOESN'T WANT THAT CRICKET...
KRIIK
...AND THAT THE CRICKET GOT AWAY!

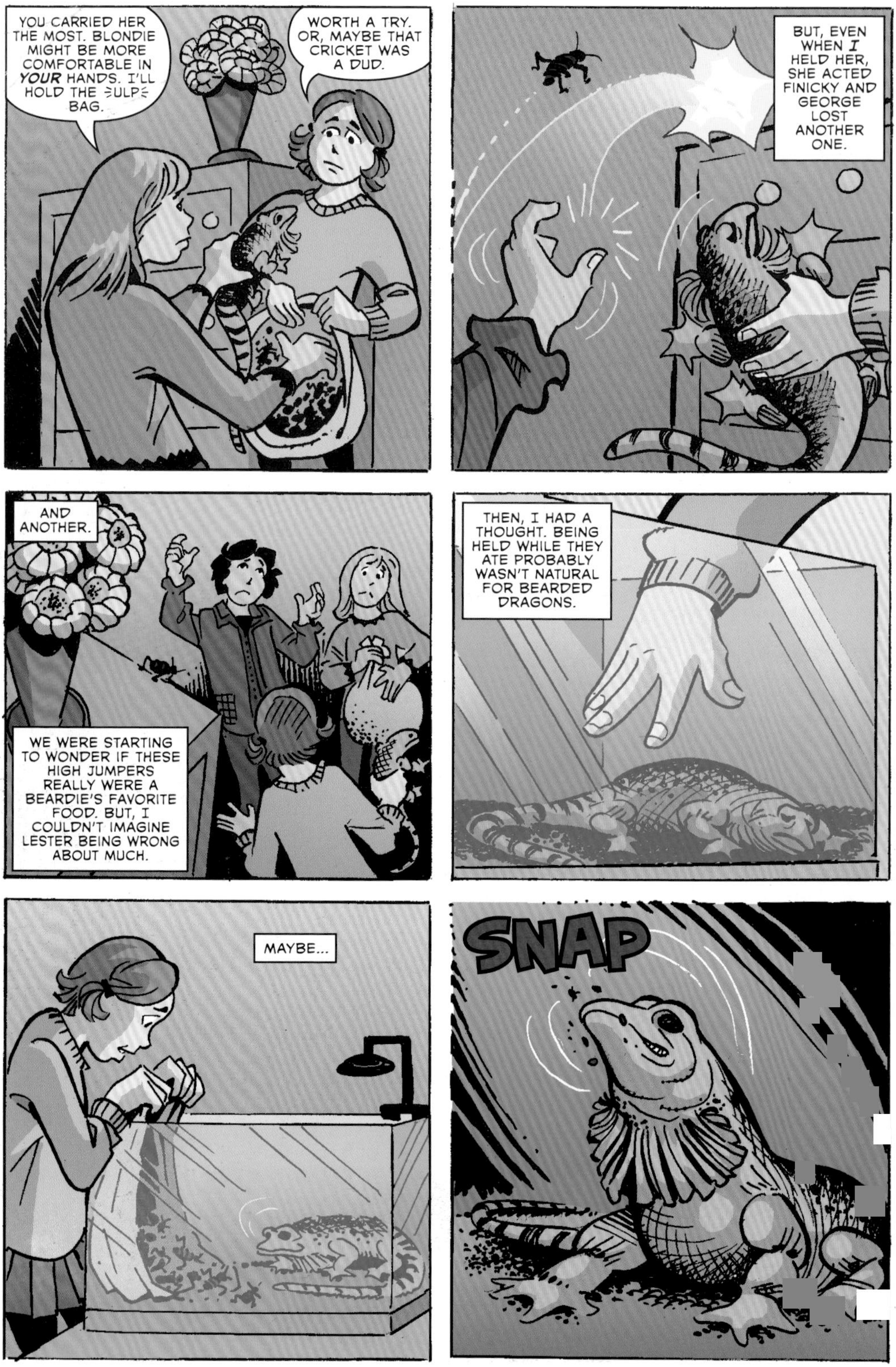
YOU CARRIED HER THE MOST. BLONDIE MIGHT BE MORE COMFORTABLE IN YOUR HANDS. I'LL HOLD THE ⋛ULP⋚ BAG.
WORTH A TRY. OR, MAYBE THAT CRICKET WAS A DUD.
BUT, EVEN WHEN I HELD HER, SHE ACTED FINICKY AND GEORGE LOST ANOTHER ONE.
AND ANOTHER.
WE WERE STARTING TO WONDER IF THESE HIGH JUMPERS REALLY WERE A BEARDIE'S FAVORITE FOOD. BUT, I COULDN'T IMAGINE LESTER BEING WRONG ABOUT MUCH.
THEN, I HAD A THOUGHT. BEING HELD WHILE THEY ATE PROBABLY WASN'T NATURAL FOR BEARDED DRAGONS.
MAYBE...
SNAP

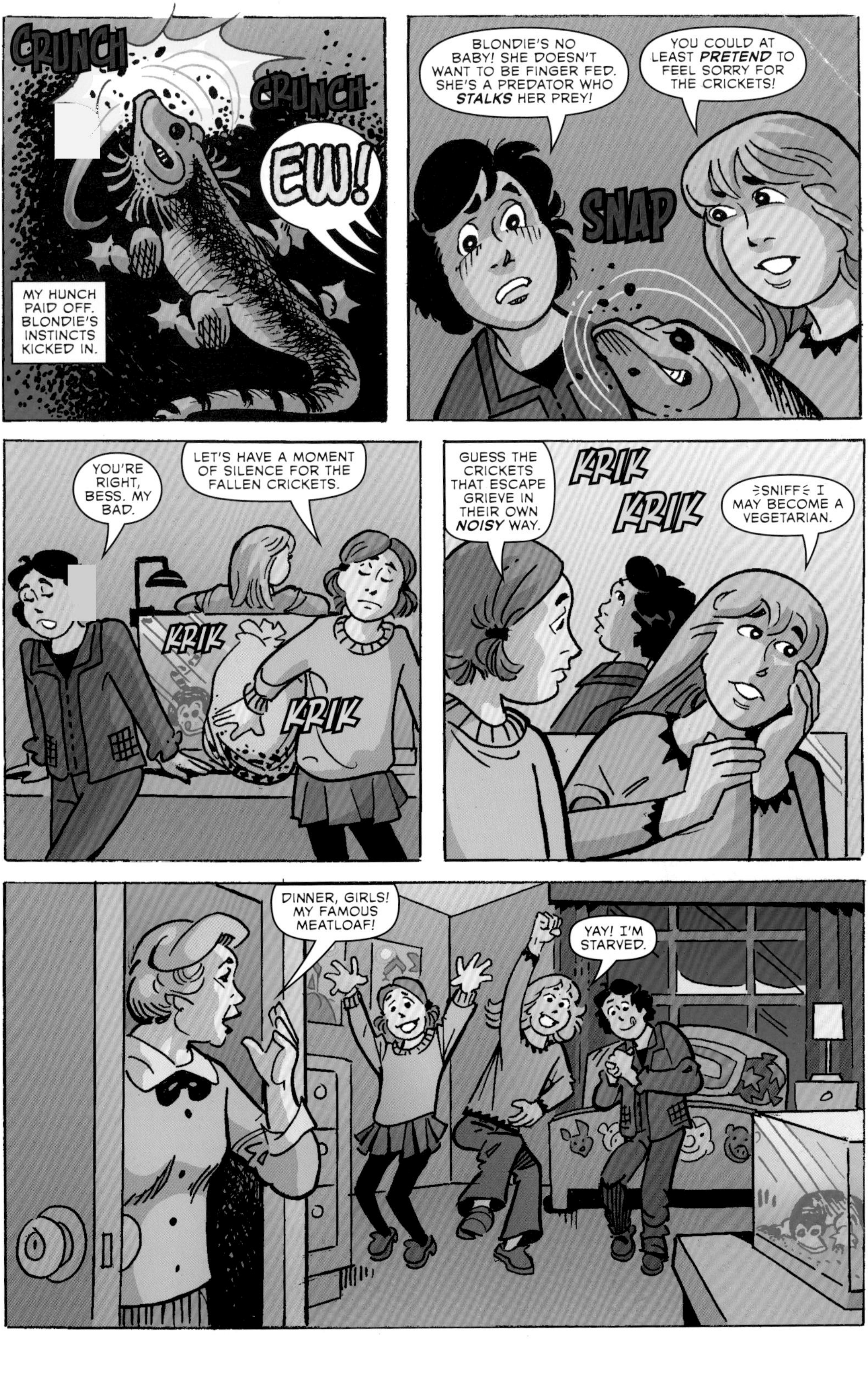
CRUNCH
CRUNCH
EW!
MY HUNCH PAID OFF. BLONDIE'S INSTINCTS KICKED IN.
BLONDIE'S NO BABY! SHE DOESN'T WANT TO BE FINGER FED. SHE'S A PREDATOR WHO STALKS HER PREY!
YOU COULD AT LEAST PRETEND TO FEEL SORRY FOR THE CRICKETS!
SNAP
YOU'RE RIGHT, BESS. MY BAD.
LET'S HAVE A MOMENT OF SILENCE FOR THE FALLEN CRICKETS.
KRIK
KRIK
GUESS THE CRICKETS THAT ESCAPE GRIEVE IN THEIR OWN NOISY WAY.
KRIK
KRIK
SNIFF I MAY BECOME A VEGETARIAN.
DINNER, GIRLS! MY FAMOUS MEATLOAF!
YAY! I'M STARVED.

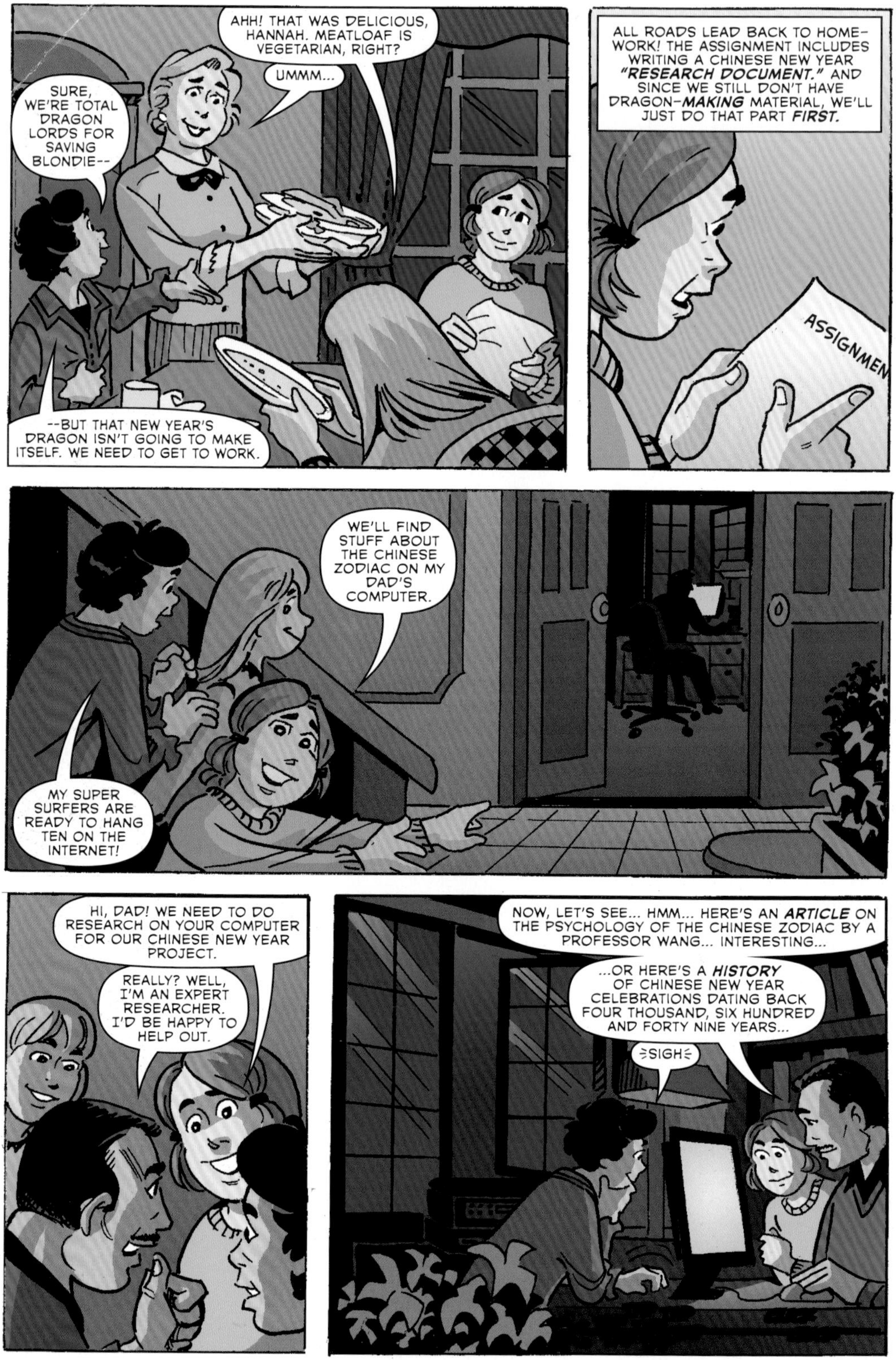
AHH! THAT WAS DELICIOUS, HANNAH. MEATLOAF IS VEGETARIAN, RIGHT?
UMMM...
SURE, WE'RE TOTAL DRAGON LORDS FOR SAVING BLONDIE--
--BUT THAT NEW YEAR'S DRAGON ISN'T GOING TO MAKE ITSELF. WE NEED TO GET TO WORK.
ALL ROADS LEAD BACK TO HOME-WORK! THE ASSIGNMENT INCLUDES WRITING A CHINESE NEW YEAR "RESEARCH DOCUMENT." AND SINCE WE STILL DON'T HAVE DRAGON-MAKING MATERIAL, WE'LL JUST DO THAT PART FIRST.
ASSIGNMEN
WE'LL FIND STUFF ABOUT THE CHINESE ZODIAC ON MY DAD'S COMPUTER.
MY SUPER SURFERS ARE READY TO HANG TEN ON THE INTERNET!
HI, DAD! WE NEED TO DO RESEARCH ON YOUR COMPUTER FOR OUR CHINESE NEW YEAR PROJECT.
REALLY? WELL, I'M AN EXPERT RESEARCHER. I'D BE HAPPY TO HELP OUT.
NOW, LET'S SEE... HMM... HERE'S AN ARTICLE ON THE PSYCHOLOGY OF THE CHINESE ZODIAC BY A PROFESSOR WANG... INTERESTING...
...OR HERE'S A HISTORY OF CHINESE NEW YEAR CELEBRATIONS DATING BACK FOUR THOUSAND, SIX HUNDRED AND FORTY NINE YEARS...
SIGH

YOU'RE A MUCH FASTER "GOOGLER" THAN NANCY'S DAD!

I KNOW, RIGHT?

THANKS, DAD, THOSE SITES SOUND *INTERESTING*, BUT WE DON'T REALLY HAVE TIME TO READ LONG ARTICLES OR A FOUR THOUSAND YEAR HISTORY, SO MAYBE...

THANKS, MR. DREW, BUT I'LL TAKE IT FROM HERE!

WHOOOAAA!

CLICK

YOU'LL HAVE TO FORGIVE MY COUSIN, MR. DREW. SHE'S A LITTLE IMPATIENT.

YOU KNOW HOW GEORGE LOVES COMPUTERS, DADDY.

I KNOW IT *NOW!*

JUST NEED THE TWELVE ANIMALS, A FEW JUICY FACTS... AND *PICTURES...*

TAPATAPTAPATAPATAP

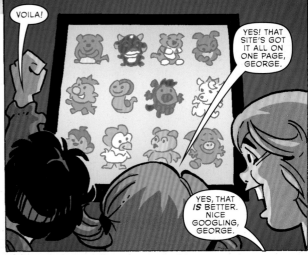

VOILA!

YES! THAT SITE'S GOT IT ALL ON ONE PAGE, GEORGE.

YES, THAT *IS* BETTER. NICE GOOGLING, GEORGE.

I CAN PRINT THAT FOR YOU. AND, I COULD CLOSE THAT WINDOW, SO YOU GIRLS DON'T GET CHILLY.

NO, THANKS, DAD! WE'RE GOOD. WE NEED TO LOOK UP OTHER STUFF ABOUT TEACHERS WHO MIGHT HAVE BOUGHT BLONDIE, AND-- WELL...

...GEORGE HAS IT UNDER CONTROL.

VKRRRRR

OKAY. ≥YAWN≤ GUESS I'LL GO READ A *BOOK* BEFORE BED. YOU KNOW BOOKS. NO MOUSE OR KEY-BOARD, A LITTLE DUSTY, BUT STILL SURPRISINGLY EFFECTIVE.

HUH? OKAY! THANKS FOR YOUR *HELP,* DAD!

SO, HERE'S THE RIVER HEIGHTS ELEMENTARY SCHOOL LIST OF TEACHERS. THERE ARE ONLY *FOUR* MALE TEACHERS.

BUT, LESTER LET IT SLIP THAT THE BUYER WASN'T "REALLY" A TEACHER. WHICH COULD MEAN AN ASSISTANT TEACHER...

THERE ARE EVEN *FEWER* OF THOSE!

TAPATAPATAP

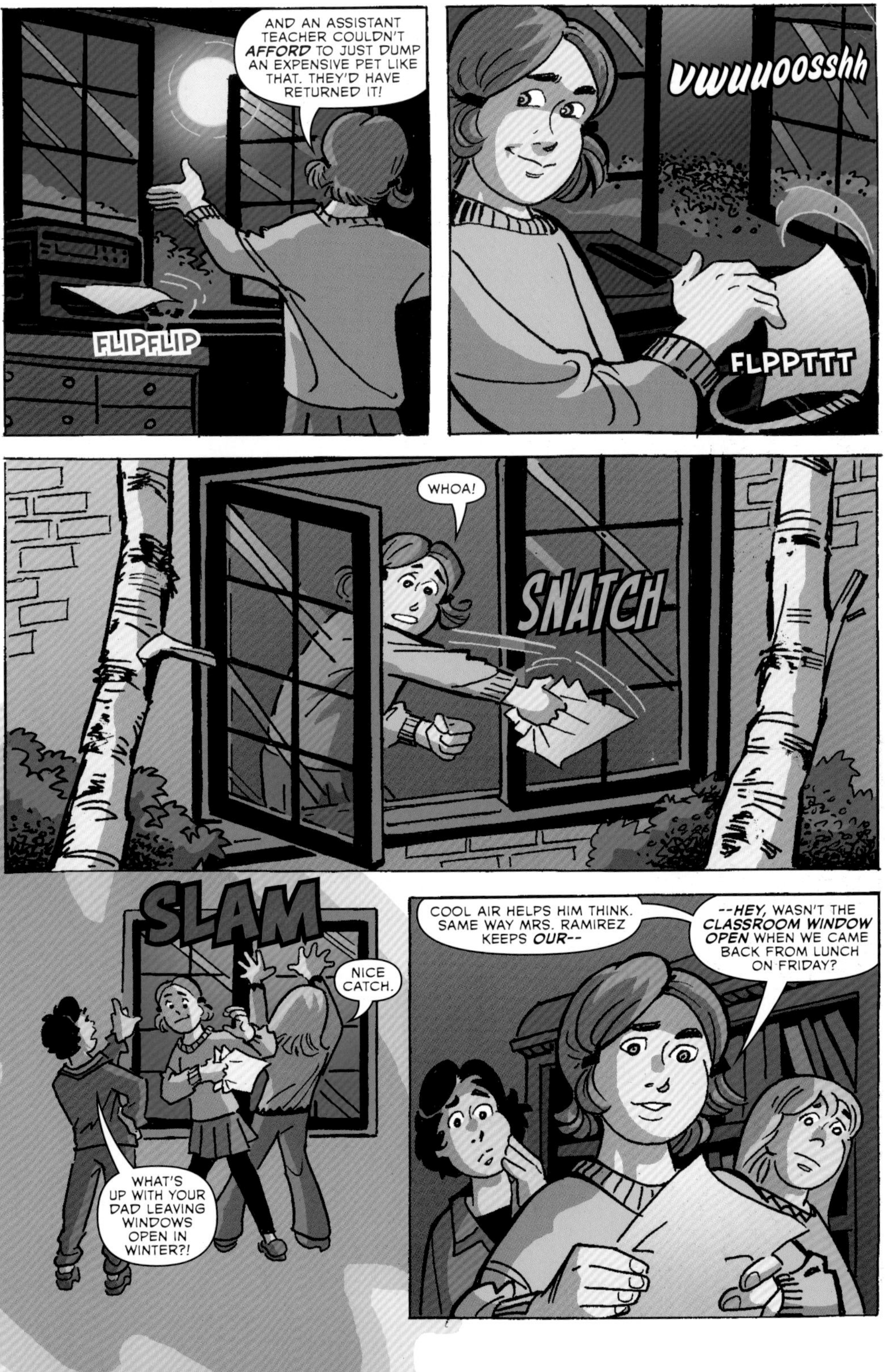
AND AN ASSISTANT TEACHER COULDN'T AFFORD TO JUST DUMP AN EXPENSIVE PET LIKE THAT. THEY'D HAVE RETURNED IT!
FLIPFLIP
VWUUOOSSHH
FLPPTTT
WHOA!
SNATCH
SLAM
NICE CATCH.
WHAT'S UP WITH YOUR DAD LEAVING WINDOWS OPEN IN WINTER?!
COOL AIR HELPS HIM THINK. SAME WAY MRS. RAMIREZ KEEPS OUR--
--HEY, WASN'T THE CLASSROOM WINDOW OPEN WHEN WE CAME BACK FROM LUNCH ON FRIDAY?

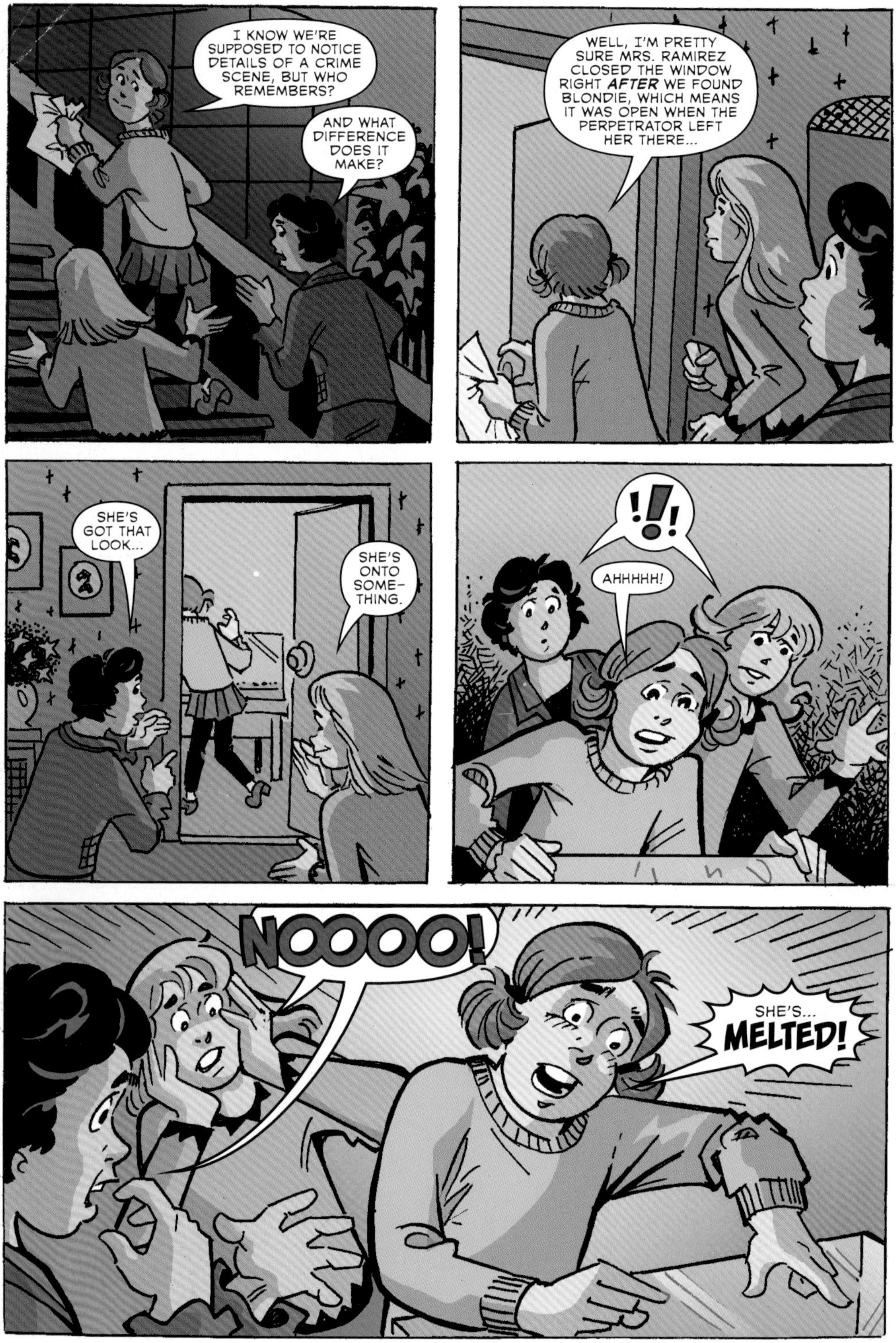

I KNOW WE'RE SUPPOSED TO NOTICE DETAILS OF A CRIME SCENE, BUT WHO REMEMBERS?
AND WHAT DIFFERENCE DOES IT MAKE?
WELL, I'M PRETTY SURE MRS. RAMIREZ CLOSED THE WINDOW RIGHT AFTER WE FOUND BLONDIE, WHICH MEANS IT WAS OPEN WHEN THE PERPETRATOR LEFT HER THERE...
SHE'S GOT THAT LOOK...
SHE'S ONTO SOME-THING.
!?!
AHHHHH!
NOOOO!
SHE'S... MELTED!

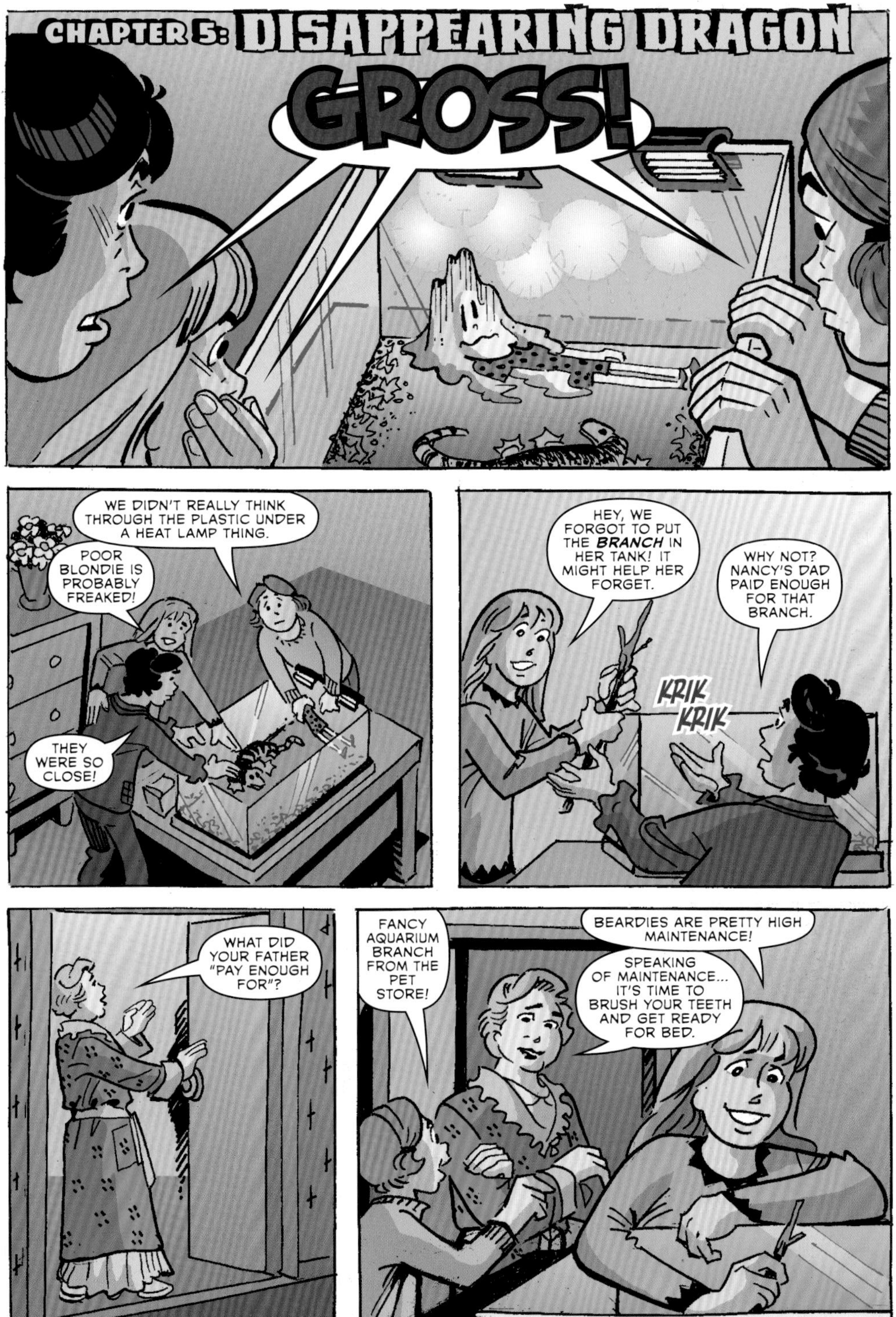
CHAPTER 5: DISAPPEARING DRAGON
GROSS!
WE DIDN'T REALLY THINK THROUGH THE PLASTIC UNDER A HEAT LAMP THING.
POOR BLONDIE IS PROBABLY FREAKED!
THEY WERE SO CLOSE!
HEY, WE FORGOT TO PUT THE BRANCH IN HER TANK! IT MIGHT HELP HER FORGET.
WHY NOT? NANCY'S DAD PAID ENOUGH FOR THAT BRANCH.
KRIK KRIK
WHAT DID YOUR FATHER "PAY ENOUGH FOR"?
FANCY AQUARIUM BRANCH FROM THE PET STORE!
BEARDIES ARE PRETTY HIGH MAINTENANCE!
SPEAKING OF MAINTENANCE... IT'S TIME TO BRUSH YOUR TEETH AND GET READY FOR BED.

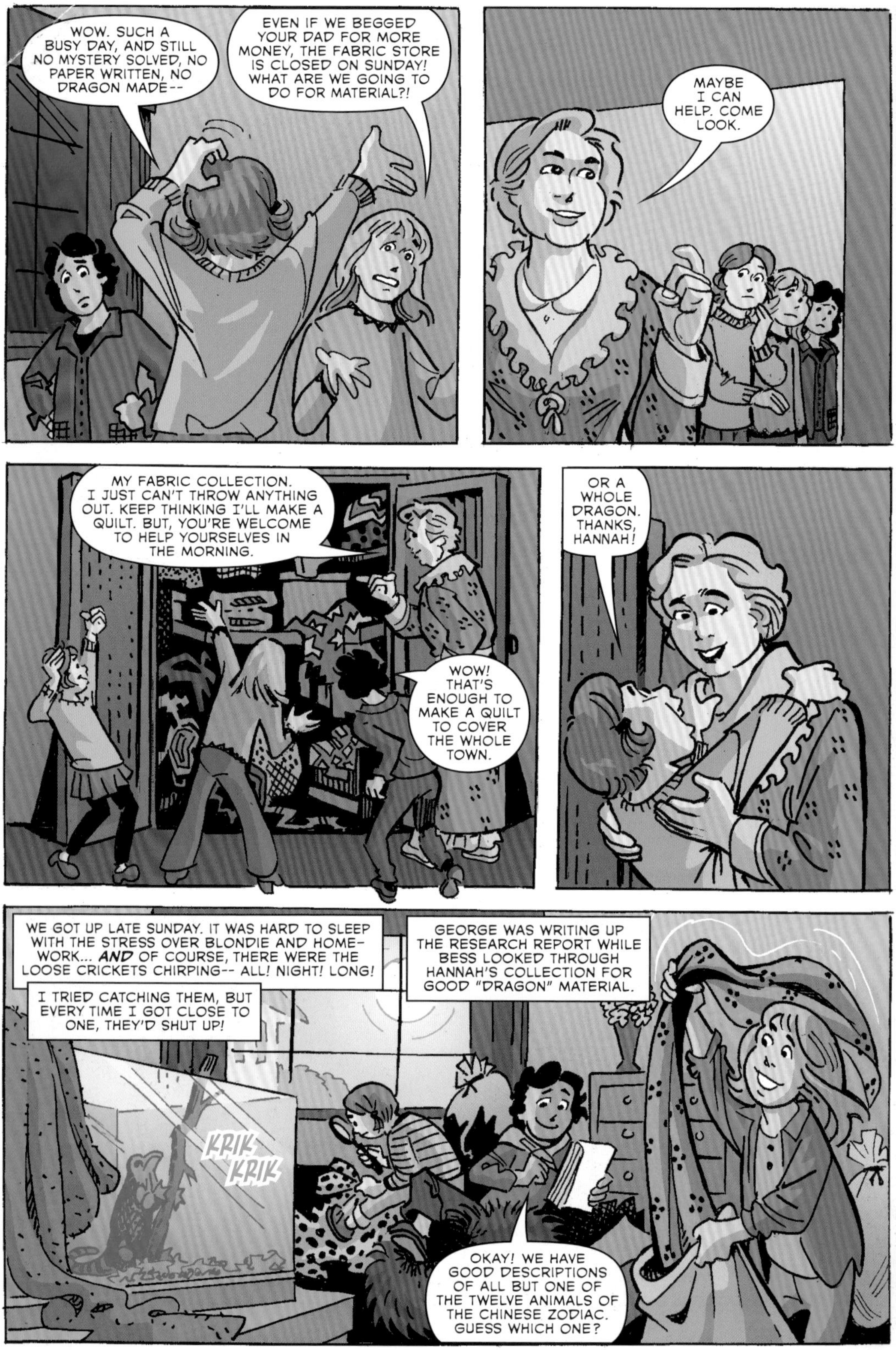
WOW. SUCH A BUSY DAY, AND STILL NO MYSTERY SOLVED, NO PAPER WRITTEN, NO DRAGON MADE--
EVEN IF WE BEGGED YOUR DAD FOR MORE MONEY, THE FABRIC STORE IS CLOSED ON SUNDAY! WHAT ARE WE GOING TO DO FOR MATERIAL?!
MAYBE I CAN HELP. COME LOOK.
MY FABRIC COLLECTION. I JUST CAN'T THROW ANYTHING OUT. KEEP THINKING I'LL MAKE A QUILT. BUT, YOU'RE WELCOME TO HELP YOURSELVES IN THE MORNING.
WOW! THAT'S ENOUGH TO MAKE A QUILT TO COVER THE WHOLE TOWN.
OR A WHOLE DRAGON. THANKS, HANNAH!
WE GOT UP LATE SUNDAY. IT WAS HARD TO SLEEP WITH THE STRESS OVER BLONDIE AND HOME-WORK... AND OF COURSE, THERE WERE THE LOOSE CRICKETS CHIRPING-- ALL! NIGHT! LONG!
I TRIED CATCHING THEM, BUT EVERY TIME I GOT CLOSE TO ONE, THEY'D SHUT UP!
GEORGE WAS WRITING UP THE RESEARCH REPORT WHILE BESS LOOKED THROUGH HANNAH'S COLLECTION FOR GOOD "DRAGON" MATERIAL.
KRIK KRIK
OKAY! WE HAVE GOOD DESCRIPTIONS OF ALL BUT ONE OF THE TWELVE ANIMALS OF THE CHINESE ZODIAC. GUESS WHICH ONE?

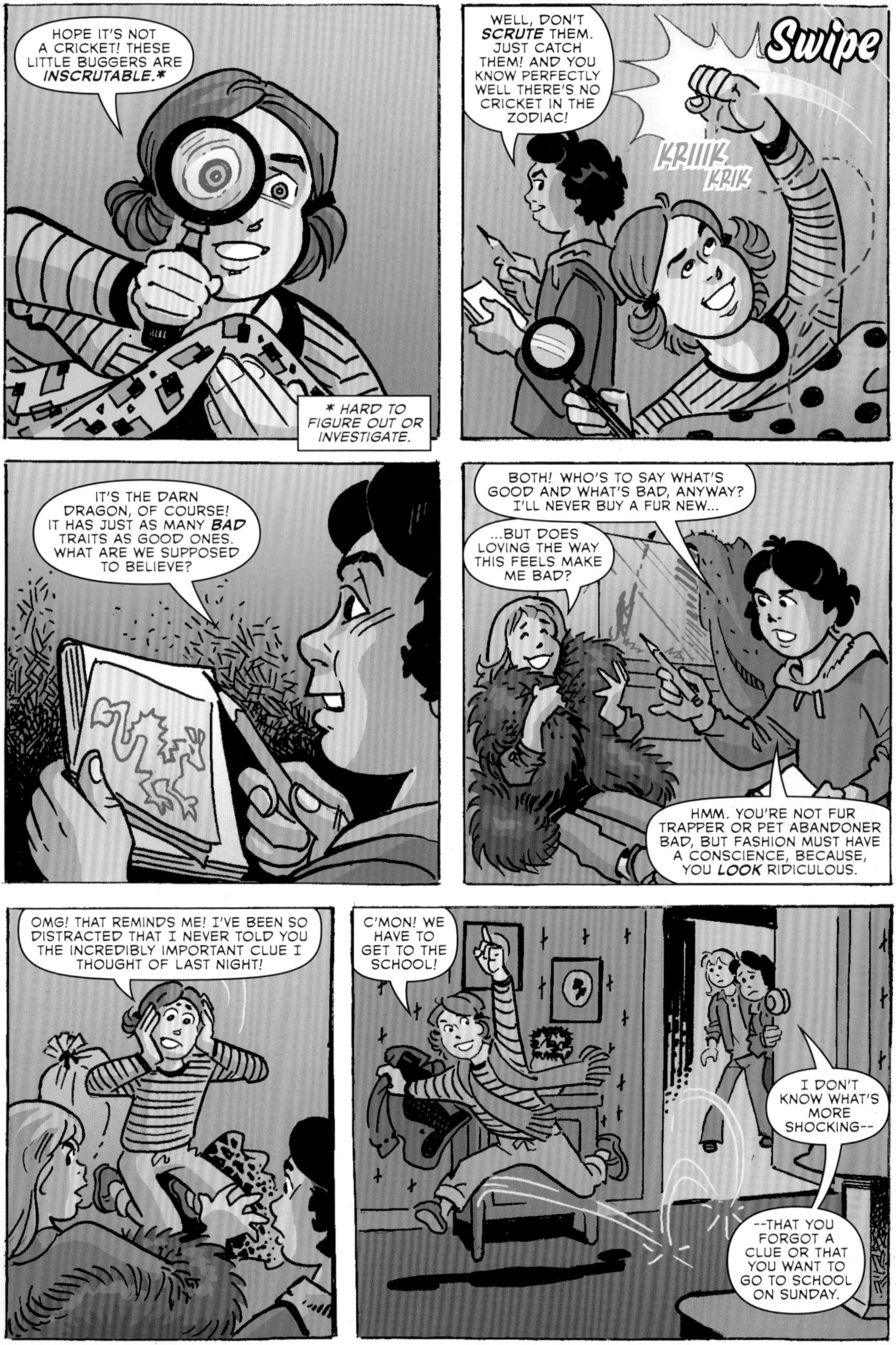
HOPE IT'S NOT A CRICKET! THESE LITTLE BUGGERS ARE *INSCRUTABLE.**
* HARD TO FIGURE OUT OR INVESTIGATE.
WELL, DON'T *SCRUTE* THEM. JUST CATCH THEM! AND YOU KNOW PERFECTLY WELL THERE'S NO CRICKET IN THE ZODIAC!
Swipe
KRIIIK KRIK
IT'S THE DARN DRAGON, OF COURSE! IT HAS JUST AS MANY *BAD* TRAITS AS GOOD ONES. WHAT ARE WE SUPPOSED TO BELIEVE?
BOTH! WHO'S TO SAY WHAT'S GOOD AND WHAT'S BAD, ANYWAY? I'LL NEVER BUY A FUR NEW...
...BUT DOES LOVING THE WAY THIS FEELS MAKE ME BAD?
HMM. YOU'RE NOT FUR TRAPPER OR PET ABANDONER BAD, BUT FASHION MUST HAVE A CONSCIENCE, BECAUSE, YOU *LOOK* RIDICULOUS.
OMG! THAT REMINDS ME! I'VE BEEN SO DISTRACTED THAT I NEVER TOLD YOU THE INCREDIBLY IMPORTANT CLUE I THOUGHT OF LAST NIGHT!
C'MON! WE HAVE TO GET TO THE SCHOOL!
I DON'T KNOW WHAT'S MORE SHOCKING--
--THAT YOU FORGOT A CLUE OR THAT YOU WANT TO GO TO SCHOOL ON SUNDAY.

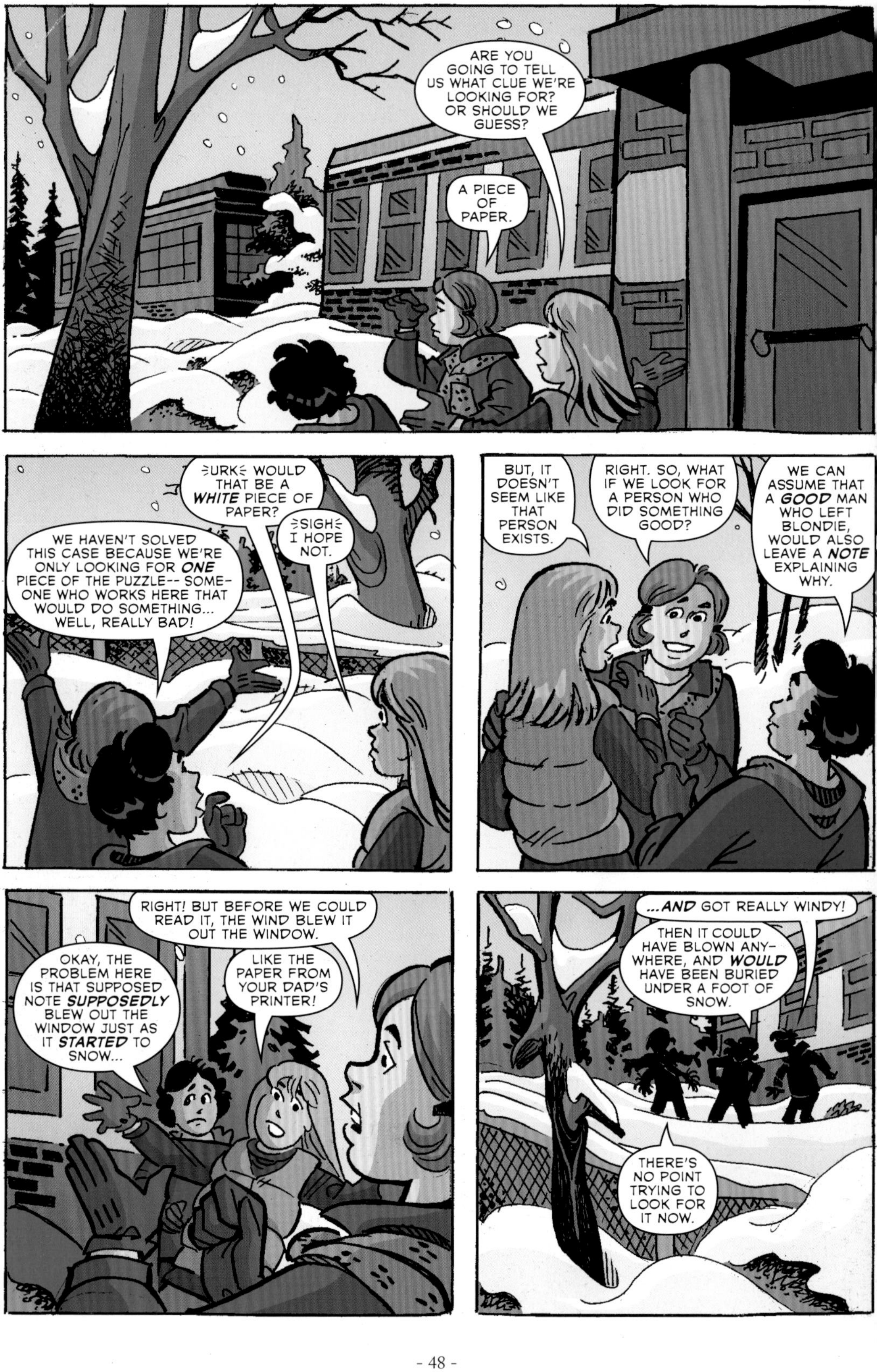

ARE YOU GOING TO TELL US WHAT CLUE WE'RE LOOKING FOR? OR SHOULD WE GUESS?
A PIECE OF PAPER.
WE HAVEN'T SOLVED THIS CASE BECAUSE WE'RE ONLY LOOKING FOR *ONE* PIECE OF THE PUZZLE-- SOMEONE WHO WORKS HERE THAT WOULD DO SOMETHING... WELL, REALLY BAD!
URK WOULD THAT BE A *WHITE* PIECE OF PAPER?
SIGH I HOPE NOT.
BUT, IT DOESN'T SEEM LIKE THAT PERSON EXISTS.
RIGHT. SO, WHAT IF WE LOOK FOR A PERSON WHO DID SOMETHING GOOD?
WE CAN ASSUME THAT A *GOOD* MAN WHO LEFT BLONDIE, WOULD ALSO LEAVE A *NOTE* EXPLAINING WHY.
RIGHT! BUT BEFORE WE COULD READ IT, THE WIND BLEW IT OUT THE WINDOW.
LIKE THE PAPER FROM YOUR DAD'S PRINTER!
OKAY, THE PROBLEM HERE IS THAT SUPPOSED NOTE *SUPPOSEDLY* BLEW OUT THE WINDOW JUST AS IT *STARTED* TO SNOW...
...AND GOT REALLY WINDY!
THEN IT COULD HAVE BLOWN ANYWHERE, AND *WOULD* HAVE BEEN BURIED UNDER A FOOT OF SNOW.
THERE'S NO POINT TRYING TO LOOK FOR IT NOW.

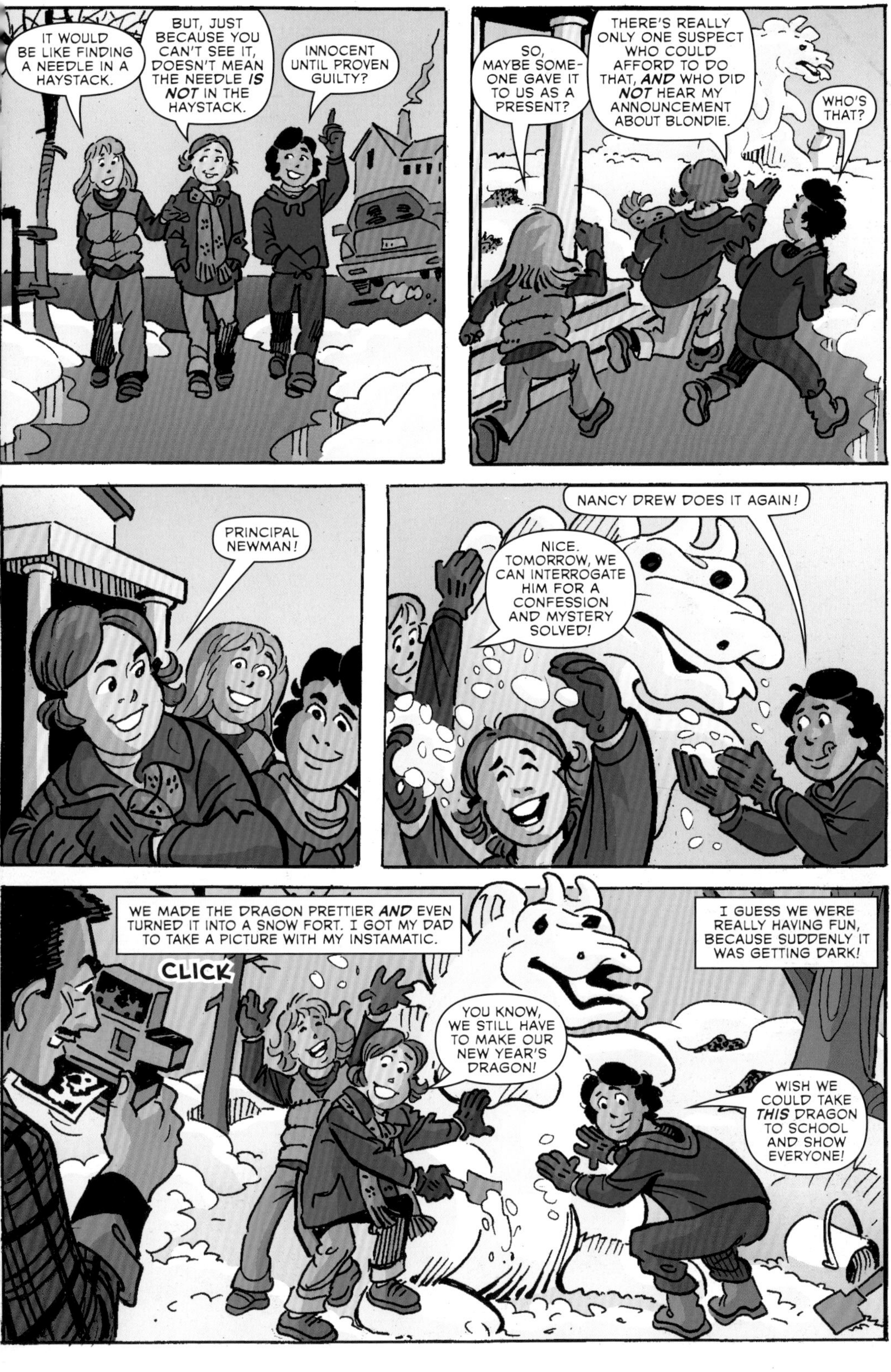
IT WOULD BE LIKE FINDING A NEEDLE IN A HAYSTACK.
BUT, JUST BECAUSE YOU CAN'T SEE IT, DOESN'T MEAN THE NEEDLE *IS* *NOT* IN THE HAYSTACK.
INNOCENT UNTIL PROVEN GUILTY?
SO, MAYBE SOME-ONE GAVE IT TO US AS A PRESENT?
THERE'S REALLY ONLY ONE SUSPECT WHO COULD AFFORD TO DO THAT, *AND* WHO DID *NOT* HEAR MY ANNOUNCEMENT ABOUT BLONDIE.
WHO'S THAT?
PRINCIPAL NEWMAN!
NANCY DREW DOES IT AGAIN!
NICE. TOMORROW, WE CAN INTERROGATE HIM FOR A CONFESSION AND MYSTERY SOLVED!
WE MADE THE DRAGON PRETTIER *AND* EVEN TURNED IT INTO A SNOW FORT. I GOT MY DAD TO TAKE A PICTURE WITH MY INSTAMATIC.
CLICK
I GUESS WE WERE REALLY HAVING FUN, BECAUSE SUDDENLY IT WAS GETTING DARK!
YOU KNOW, WE STILL HAVE TO MAKE OUR NEW YEAR'S DRAGON!
WISH WE COULD TAKE *THIS* DRAGON TO SCHOOL AND SHOW EVERYONE!

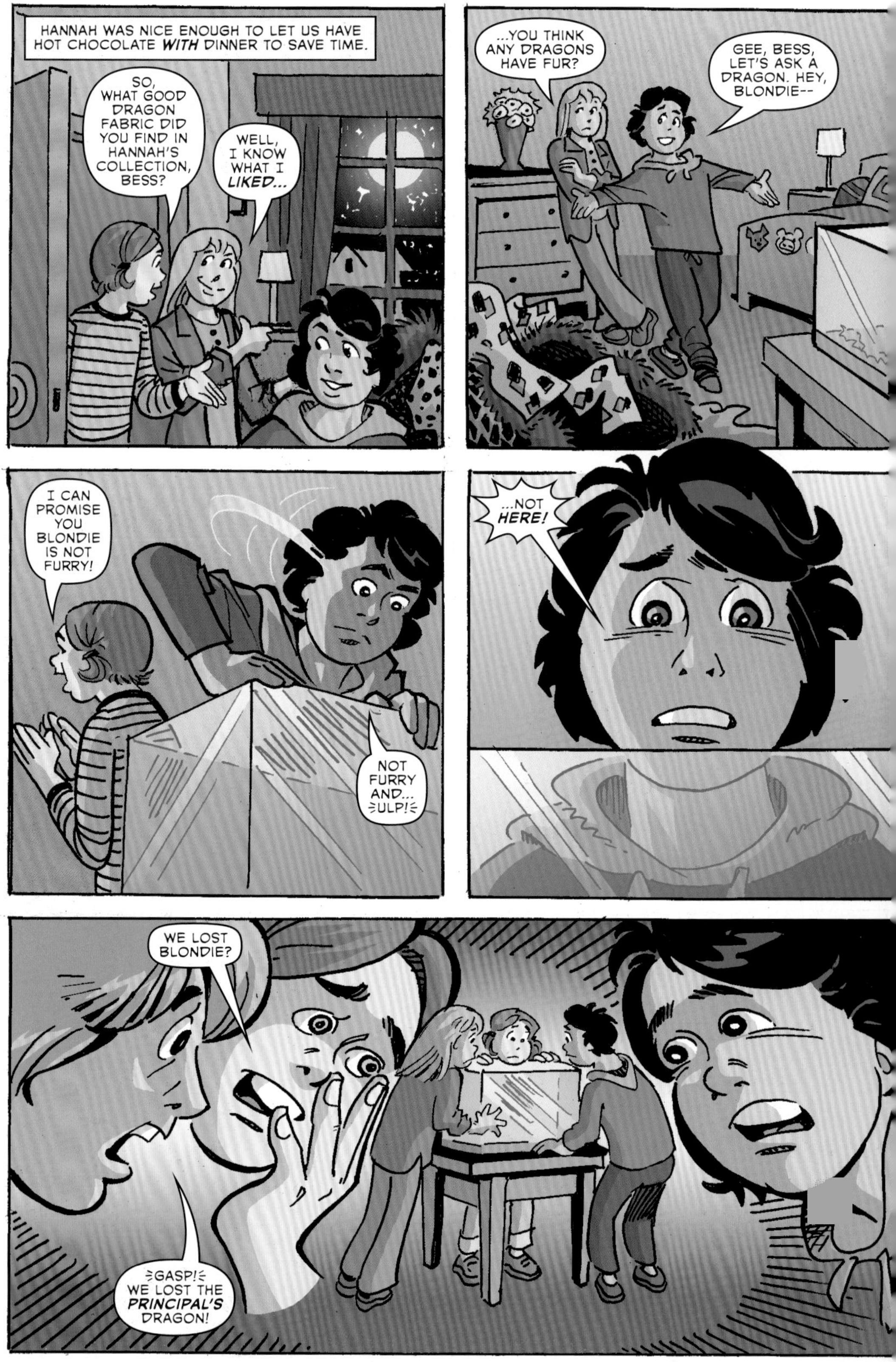
HANNAH WAS NICE ENOUGH TO LET US HAVE HOT CHOCOLATE WITH DINNER TO SAVE TIME.
SO, WHAT GOOD DRAGON FABRIC DID YOU FIND IN HANNAH'S COLLECTION, BESS?
WELL, I KNOW WHAT I LIKED...
...YOU THINK ANY DRAGONS HAVE FUR?
GEE, BESS, LET'S ASK A DRAGON. HEY, BLONDIE--
I CAN PROMISE YOU BLONDIE IS NOT FURRY!
NOT FURRY AND... ULP!
...NOT HERE!
WE LOST BLONDIE?
GASP! WE LOST THE PRINCIPAL'S DRAGON!

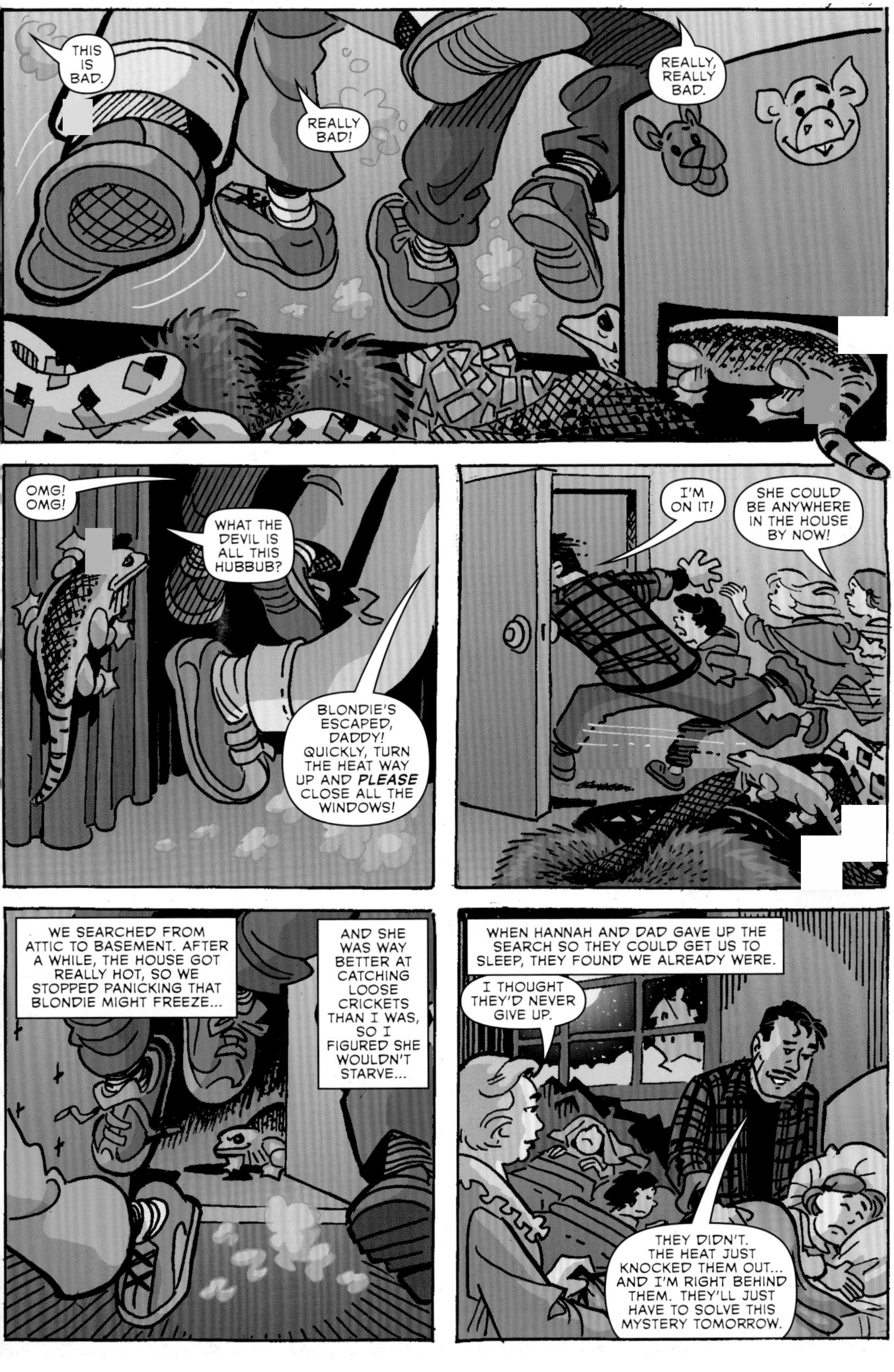
THIS IS BAD.
REALLY BAD!
REALLY, REALLY BAD.
OMG! OMG!
WHAT THE DEVIL IS ALL THIS HUBBUB?
BLONDIE'S ESCAPED, DADDY! QUICKLY, TURN THE HEAT WAY UP AND PLEASE CLOSE ALL THE WINDOWS!
I'M ON IT!
SHE COULD BE ANYWHERE IN THE HOUSE BY NOW!
WE SEARCHED FROM ATTIC TO BASEMENT. AFTER A WHILE, THE HOUSE GOT REALLY HOT, SO WE STOPPED PANICKING THAT BLONDIE MIGHT FREEZE...
AND SHE WAS WAY BETTER AT CATCHING LOOSE CRICKETS THAN I WAS, SO I FIGURED SHE WOULDN'T STARVE...
WHEN HANNAH AND DAD GAVE UP THE SEARCH SO THEY COULD GET US TO SLEEP, THEY FOUND WE ALREADY WERE.
I THOUGHT THEY'D NEVER GIVE UP.
THEY DIDN'T. THE HEAT JUST KNOCKED THEM OUT... AND I'M RIGHT BEHIND THEM. THEY'LL JUST HAVE TO SOLVE THIS MYSTERY TOMORROW.

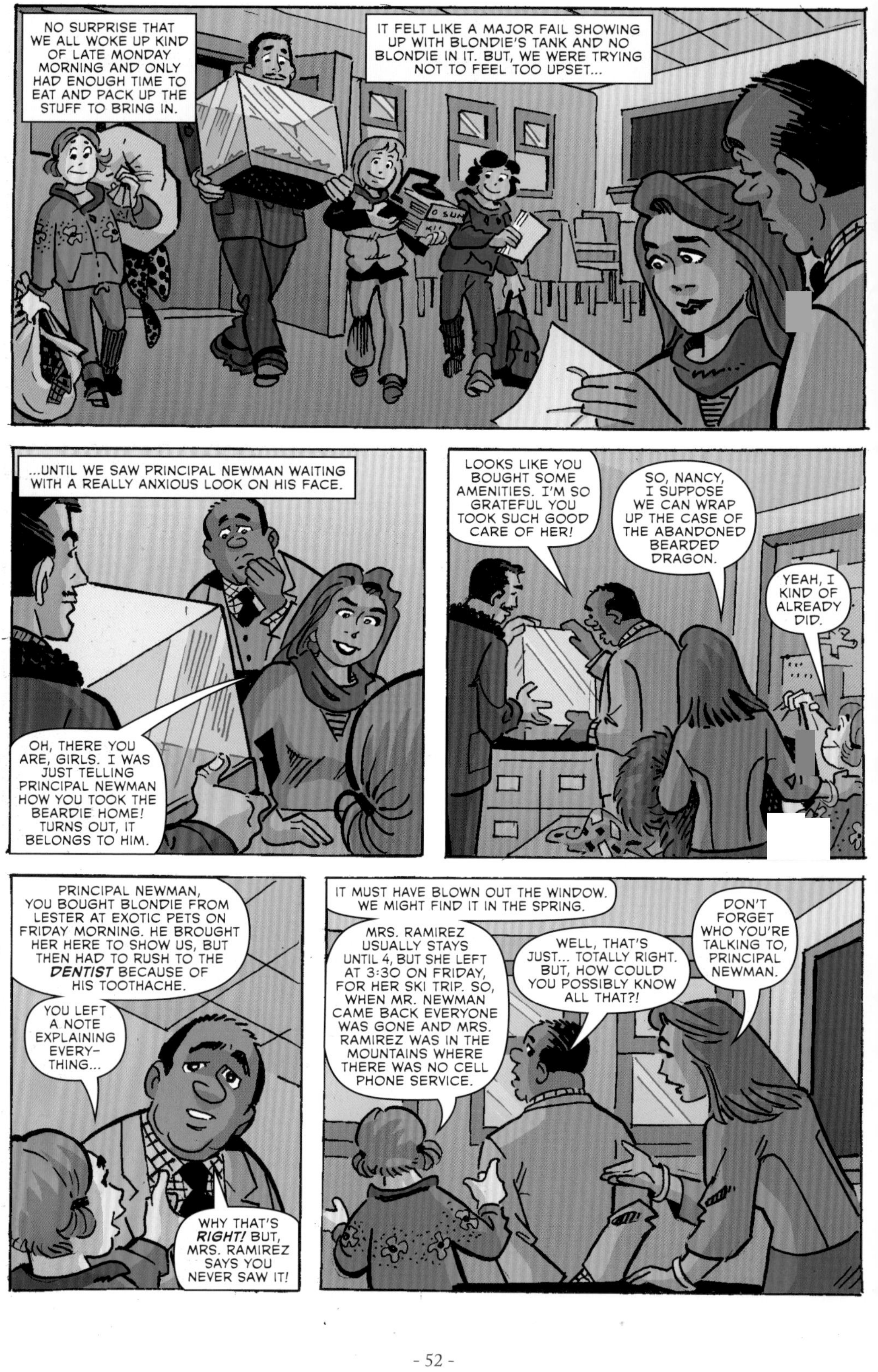
NO SURPRISE THAT WE ALL WOKE UP KIND OF LATE MONDAY MORNING AND ONLY HAD ENOUGH TIME TO EAT AND PACK UP THE STUFF TO BRING IN.
IT FELT LIKE A MAJOR FAIL SHOWING UP WITH BLONDIE'S TANK AND NO BLONDIE IN IT. BUT, WE WERE TRYING NOT TO FEEL TOO UPSET...
...UNTIL WE SAW PRINCIPAL NEWMAN WAITING WITH A REALLY ANXIOUS LOOK ON HIS FACE.
OH, THERE YOU ARE, GIRLS. I WAS JUST TELLING PRINCIPAL NEWMAN HOW YOU TOOK THE BEARDIE HOME! TURNS OUT, IT BELONGS TO HIM.
LOOKS LIKE YOU BOUGHT SOME AMENITIES. I'M SO GRATEFUL YOU TOOK SUCH GOOD CARE OF HER!
SO, NANCY, I SUPPOSE WE CAN WRAP UP THE CASE OF THE ABANDONED BEARDED DRAGON.
YEAH, I KIND OF ALREADY DID.
PRINCIPAL NEWMAN, YOU BOUGHT BLONDIE FROM LESTER AT EXOTIC PETS ON FRIDAY MORNING. HE BROUGHT HER HERE TO SHOW US, BUT THEN HAD TO RUSH TO THE *DENTIST* BECAUSE OF HIS TOOTHACHE.
YOU LEFT A NOTE EXPLAINING EVERY-THING...
WHY THAT'S *RIGHT!* BUT, MRS. RAMIREZ SAYS YOU NEVER SAW IT!
IT MUST HAVE BLOWN OUT THE WINDOW. WE MIGHT FIND IT IN THE SPRING.
MRS. RAMIREZ USUALLY STAYS UNTIL 4, BUT SHE LEFT AT 3:30 ON FRIDAY, FOR HER SKI TRIP. SO, WHEN MR. NEWMAN CAME BACK EVERYONE WAS GONE AND MRS. RAMIREZ WAS IN THE MOUNTAINS WHERE THERE WAS NO CELL PHONE SERVICE.
WELL, THAT'S JUST... TOTALLY RIGHT. BUT, HOW COULD YOU POSSIBLY KNOW ALL THAT?!
DON'T FORGET WHO YOU'RE TALKING TO, PRINCIPAL NEWMAN.

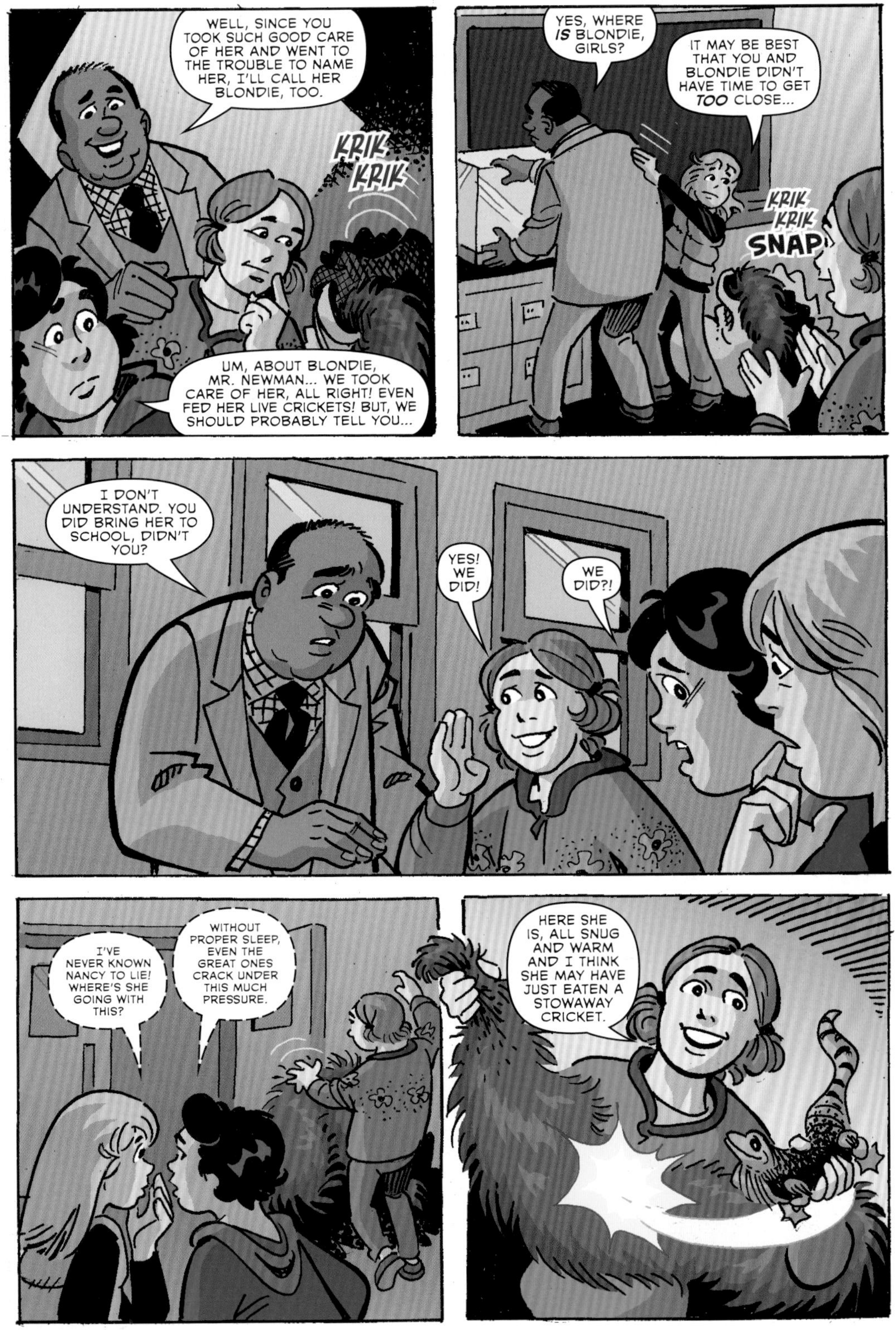
WELL, SINCE YOU TOOK SUCH GOOD CARE OF HER AND WENT TO THE TROUBLE TO NAME HER, I'LL CALL HER BLONDIE, TOO.
KRIK KRIK
UM, ABOUT BLONDIE, MR. NEWMAN... WE TOOK CARE OF HER, ALL RIGHT! EVEN FED HER LIVE CRICKETS! BUT, WE SHOULD PROBABLY TELL YOU...
YES, WHERE *IS* BLONDIE, GIRLS?
IT MAY BE BEST THAT YOU AND BLONDIE DIDN'T HAVE TIME TO GET *TOO* CLOSE...
KRIK KRIK
SNAP
I DON'T UNDERSTAND. YOU DID BRING HER TO SCHOOL, DIDN'T YOU?
YES! WE DID!
WE DID?!
I'VE NEVER KNOWN NANCY TO LIE! WHERE'S SHE GOING WITH THIS?
WITHOUT PROPER SLEEP, EVEN THE GREAT ONES CRACK UNDER THIS MUCH PRESSURE.
HERE SHE IS, ALL SNUG AND WARM AND I THINK SHE MAY HAVE JUST EATEN A STOWAWAY CRICKET.

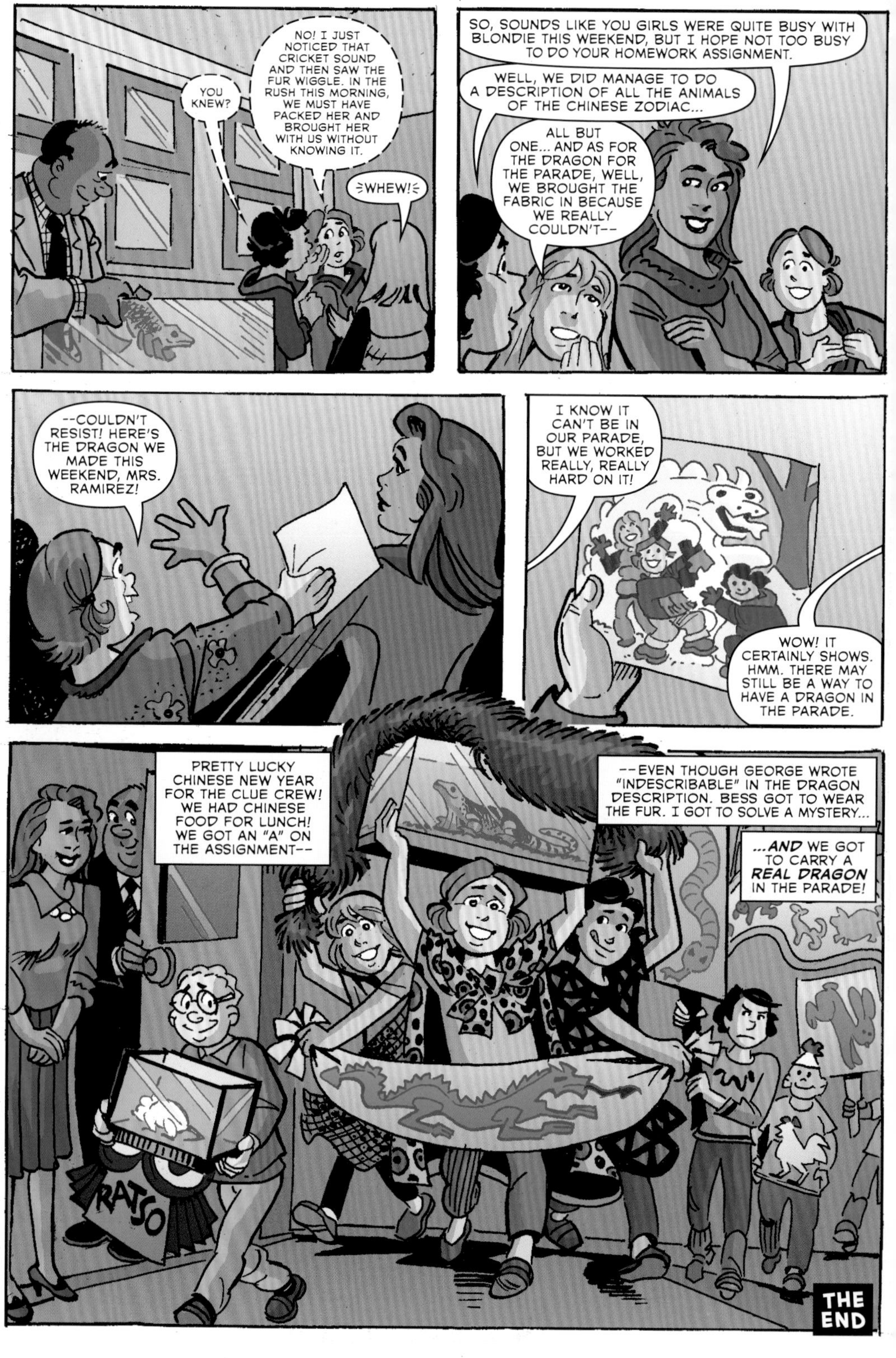
YOU KNEW?
NO! I JUST NOTICED THAT CRICKET SOUND AND THEN SAW THE FUR WIGGLE. IN THE RUSH THIS MORNING, WE MUST HAVE PACKED HER AND BROUGHT HER WITH US WITHOUT KNOWING IT.
WHEW!
SO, SOUNDS LIKE YOU GIRLS WERE QUITE BUSY WITH BLONDIE THIS WEEKEND, BUT I HOPE NOT TOO BUSY TO DO YOUR HOMEWORK ASSIGNMENT.
WELL, WE DID MANAGE TO DO A DESCRIPTION OF ALL THE ANIMALS OF THE CHINESE ZODIAC...
ALL BUT ONE... AND AS FOR THE DRAGON FOR THE PARADE, WELL, WE BROUGHT THE FABRIC IN BECAUSE WE REALLY COULDN'T--
--COULDN'T RESIST! HERE'S THE DRAGON WE MADE THIS WEEKEND, MRS. RAMIREZ!
I KNOW IT CAN'T BE IN OUR PARADE, BUT WE WORKED REALLY, REALLY HARD ON IT!
WOW! IT CERTAINLY SHOWS. HMM. THERE MAY STILL BE A WAY TO HAVE A DRAGON IN THE PARADE.
PRETTY LUCKY CHINESE NEW YEAR FOR THE CLUE CREW! WE HAD CHINESE FOOD FOR LUNCH! WE GOT AN "A" ON THE ASSIGNMENT--
--EVEN THOUGH GEORGE WROTE "INDESCRIBABLE" IN THE DRAGON DESCRIPTION. BESS GOT TO WEAR THE FUR. I GOT TO SOLVE A MYSTERY...
...AND WE GOT TO CARRY A REAL DRAGON IN THE PARADE!
RATSO
THE END

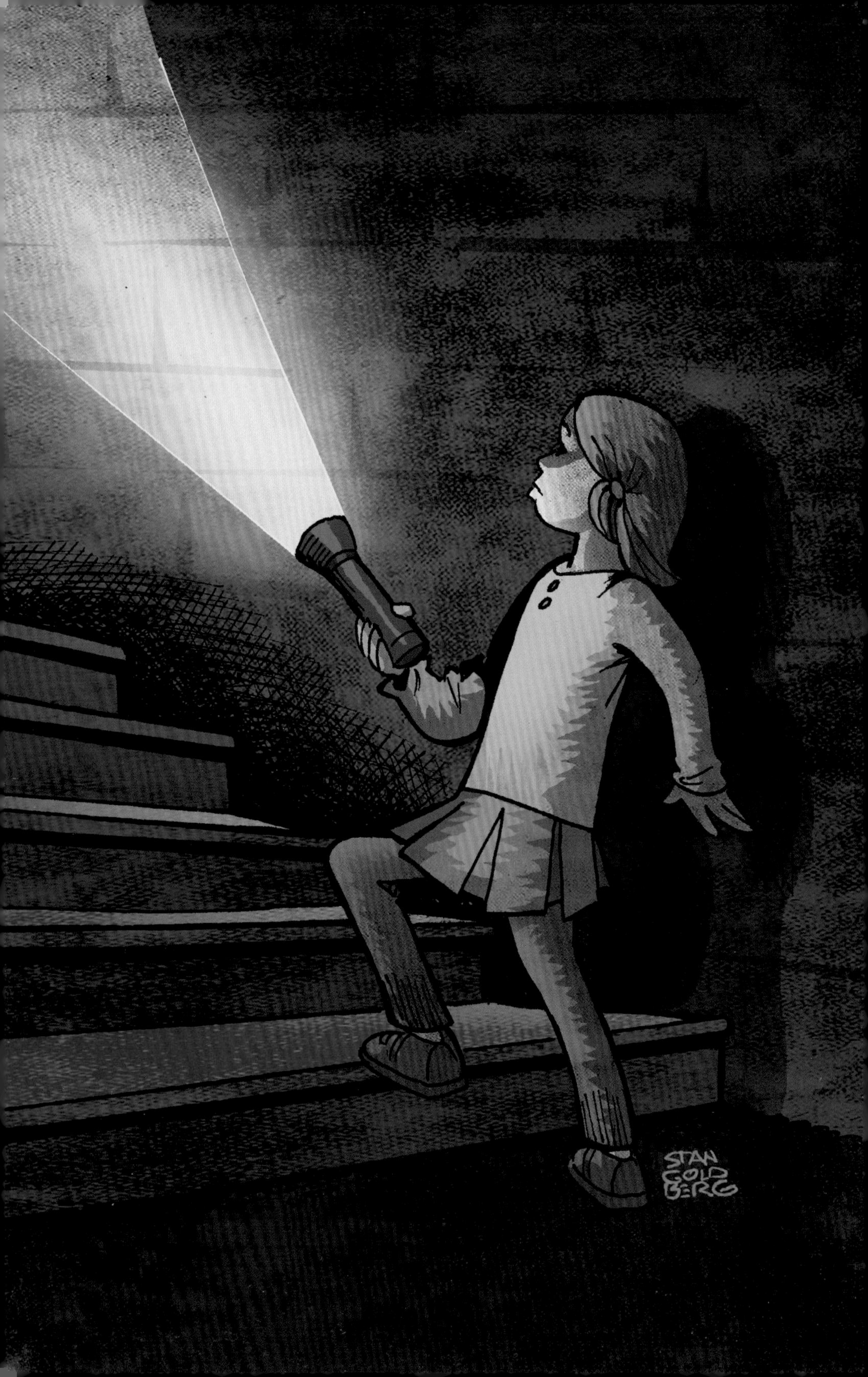
STAN
GOLD
BERG

WATCH OUT FOR PAPERCUTZ™

Welcome to the totally thrilling third NANCY DREW AND THE CLUE CREW graphic novel from Papercutz, the perpetually perplexed and puzzled people dedicated to publishing great graphic novels for all ages. I'm Jim Salicrup, the Editor-in-Chief and magnifying glass maintainer, and I'm happy that you've picked up this Papercutz graphic novel.

We've got BIG NEWS for Nancy Drew fans! Due to popular demand, we'll soon be publishing another NANCY DREW title, this one featuring the 18 year old Nancy! So many of you have written to us asking where to find many of the out-of-print earlier NANCY DREW graphic novels by Stefan Petrucha (and later, Sarah Kinney) and Sho Murase (and a couple drawn by Vaughn Ross), that we realized it might just be a good idea to bring them back into print! Of course, many are still available directly from us via mail order or as ebooks, but now we have a new series that will be available in bookstores. We'll be calling it NANCY DREW DIARIES, and each volume will feature two complete graphic novels from the earlier series.

In the meantime, we just had to show you (on the opposite page) this beautiful bit of artwork, drawn by Stan Goldberg and colored by Laurie E. Smith, that was used on the free NANCY DREW AND THE CLUE CREW tote bags given away recently at the Book Expo: America. The bags were so popular they were all gone in a matter of hours! I don't even have one, but I think I know where Jesse Post, our Director of Marketing, may be hiding a few!

More BIG NEWS! If you're at all familiar with www.stardoll.com, then you already know what a super-cool website that is—especially if you're into fashion! Well, Papercutz has managed to sign a deal for us to create STARDOLL graphic novels, and they're like nothing you've ever seen before! In fact, we're offering a sneak preview of the first graphic novel, "Secrets & Dreams" on the following pages! What could possibly be better than that?

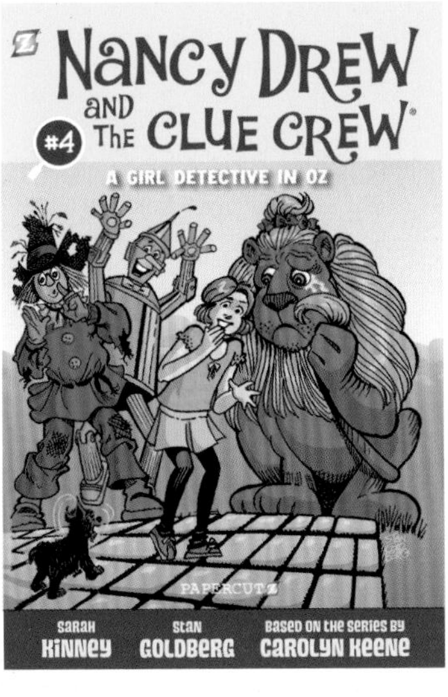

Nancy Drew
and The Clue Crew
#4
A Girl Detective in Oz
Papercutz
Sarah Kinney
Stan Goldberg
Based on the series by Carolyn Keene

Even more BIG NEWS! Well, since I asked, I'll answer that the very next NANCY DREW AND THE CLUE CREW is really super-special! The title tells you everything you need to know, so be sure not to miss: NANCY DREW AND THE CLUE CREW #4 "A Girl Detective in Oz." (Hint: We're not talking about Nancy going to Australia!)

Thanks,

Jim

STAY IN TOUCH!

EMAIL:	salicrup@papercutz.com
WEB:	www.papercutz.com
TWITTER:	@papercutzgn
FACEBOOK:	PAPERCUTZGRAPHICNOVELS
SNAIL MAIL:	Papercutz, 160 Broadway, Suite 700, East Wing, New York, NY 10038

An Exclusive Preview!

stardoll™

Secrets & Dreams

by JayJay Jackson

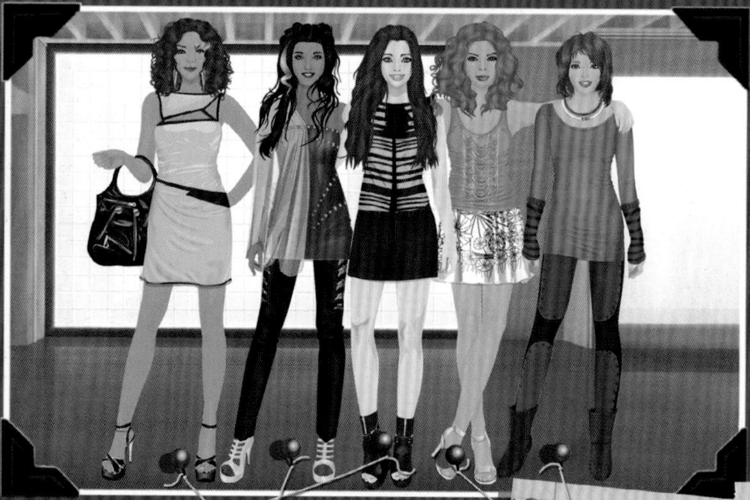

Claire Leo

Fashion Style:
Casual, Fashion Forward
Dream:
To be a Fashion Designer

Ashley Archer

Fashion Style:
Feminine, Athletic
Dream:
To be a Fashion Business Manager

Kaya Reynard

Fashion Style:
Eclectic, Loves trying different styles
Dream:
To be an Interior Decorator

Sue-Ni MacDuffie

Fashion Style:
Asian inspired, Feminine, Pretty
Dream:
To be a Fashion Buyer

Ruby Zara

Fashion Style:
80's Vintage, Geek Chic
Dream:
Developing Fashion Technologies

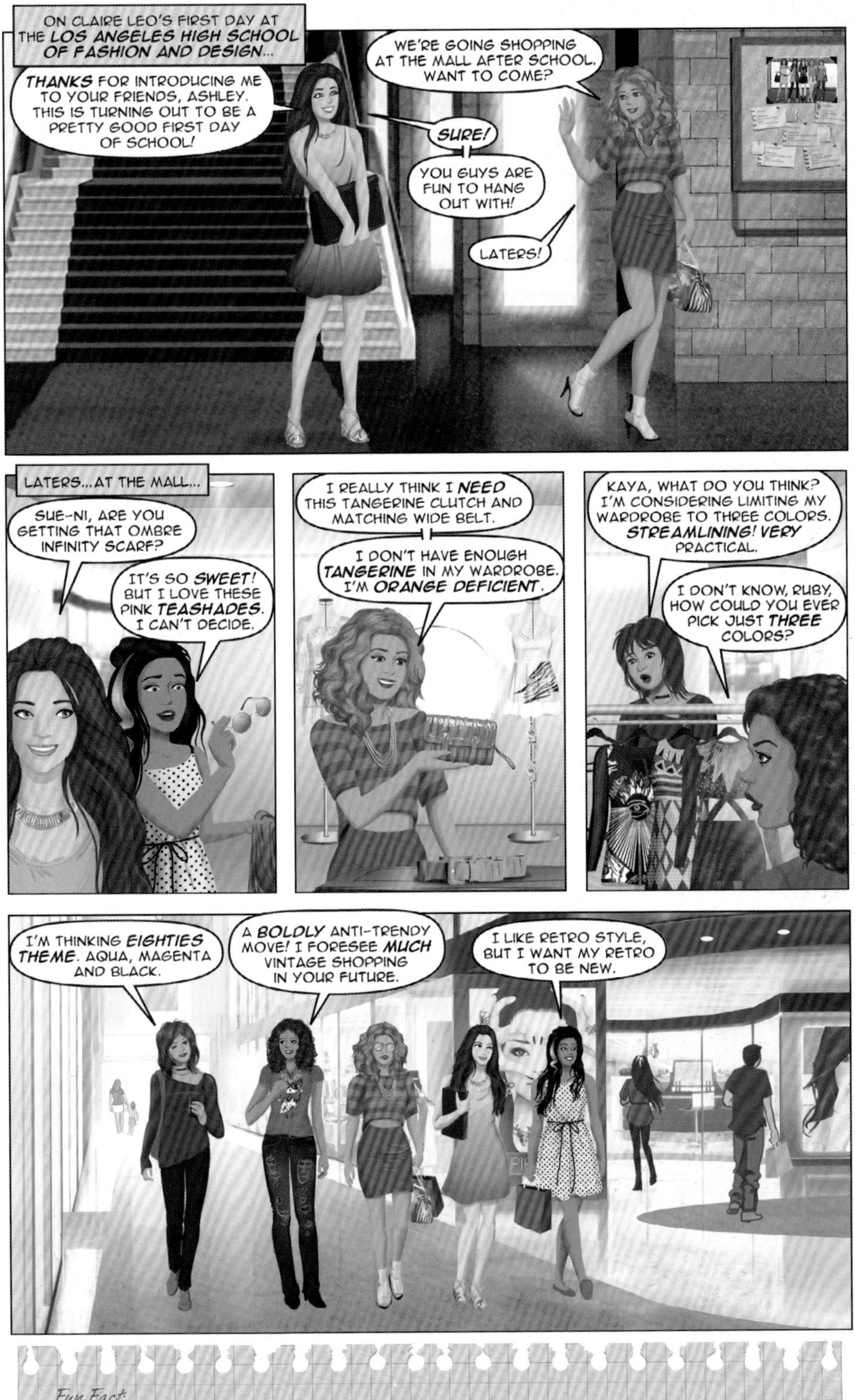

ON CLAIRE LEO'S FIRST DAY AT THE LOS ANGELES HIGH SCHOOL OF FASHION AND DESIGN...
THANKS FOR INTRODUCING ME TO YOUR FRIENDS, ASHLEY. THIS IS TURNING OUT TO BE A PRETTY GOOD FIRST DAY OF SCHOOL!
WE'RE GOING SHOPPING AT THE MALL AFTER SCHOOL. WANT TO COME?
SURE!
YOU GUYS ARE FUN TO HANG OUT WITH!
LATERS!
LATERS...AT THE MALL...
SUE-NI, ARE YOU GETTING THAT OMBRE INFINITY SCARF?
IT'S SO SWEET! BUT I LOVE THESE PINK TEASHADES. I CAN'T DECIDE.
I REALLY THINK I NEED THIS TANGERINE CLUTCH AND MATCHING WIDE BELT.
I DON'T HAVE ENOUGH TANGERINE IN MY WARDROBE. I'M ORANGE DEFICIENT.
KAYA, WHAT DO YOU THINK? I'M CONSIDERING LIMITING MY WARDROBE TO THREE COLORS. STREAMLINING! VERY PRACTICAL.
I DON'T KNOW, RUBY, HOW COULD YOU EVER PICK JUST THREE COLORS?
I'M THINKING EIGHTIES THEME. AQUA, MAGENTA AND BLACK.
A BOLDLY ANTI-TRENDY MOVE! I FORESEE MUCH VINTAGE SHOPPING IN YOUR FUTURE.
I LIKE RETRO STYLE, BUT I WANT MY RETRO TO BE NEW.

Fun Fact:

Claire Leo has dreamed of being a fashion designer her whole life and has created many spectacular outfits for her sister's dolls.

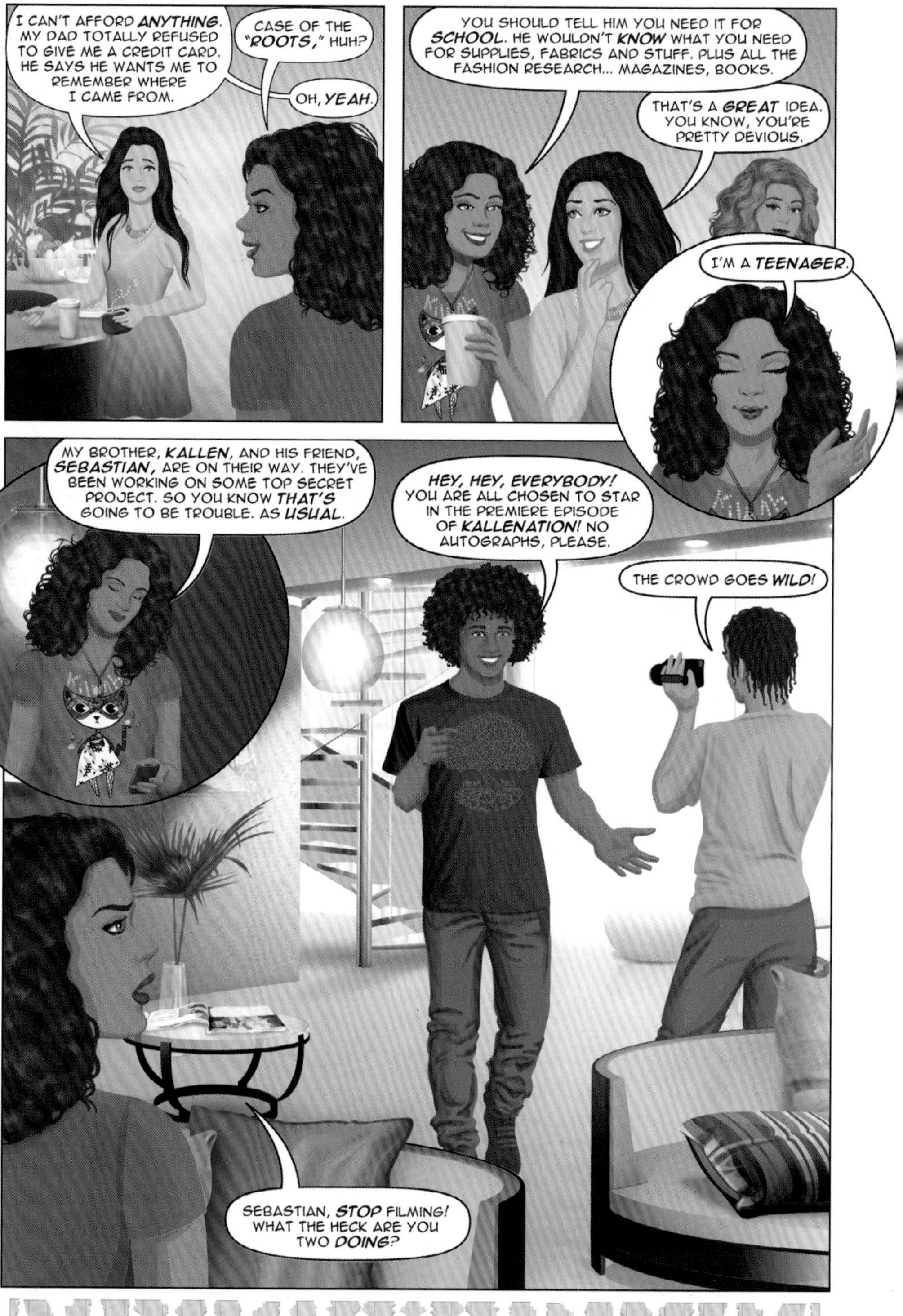
I CAN'T AFFORD ANYTHING. MY DAD TOTALLY REFUSED TO GIVE ME A CREDIT CARD. HE SAYS HE WANTS ME TO REMEMBER WHERE I CAME FROM.
CASE OF THE "ROOTS," HUH?
OH, YEAH.
YOU SHOULD TELL HIM YOU NEED IT FOR SCHOOL. HE WOULDN'T KNOW WHAT YOU NEED FOR SUPPLIES, FABRICS AND STUFF. PLUS ALL THE FASHION RESEARCH... MAGAZINES, BOOKS.
THAT'S A GREAT IDEA. YOU KNOW, YOU'RE PRETTY DEVIOUS.
I'M A TEENAGER.
MY BROTHER, KALLEN, AND HIS FRIEND, SEBASTIAN, ARE ON THEIR WAY. THEY'VE BEEN WORKING ON SOME TOP SECRET PROJECT. SO YOU KNOW THAT'S GOING TO BE TROUBLE. AS USUAL.
HEY, HEY, EVERYBODY! YOU ARE ALL CHOSEN TO STAR IN THE PREMIERE EPISODE OF KALLENATION! NO AUTOGRAPHS, PLEASE.
THE CROWD GOES WILD!
SEBASTIAN, STOP FILMING! WHAT THE HECK ARE YOU TWO DOING?

Fun Fact:

Kaya Reynard loves to keep up on the latest of everything in the fashion world. Her brother, Kallen, is more of a pop culture junkie. His best friend, Sebastian Rios, is always up for all the crazy adventures they dream up.

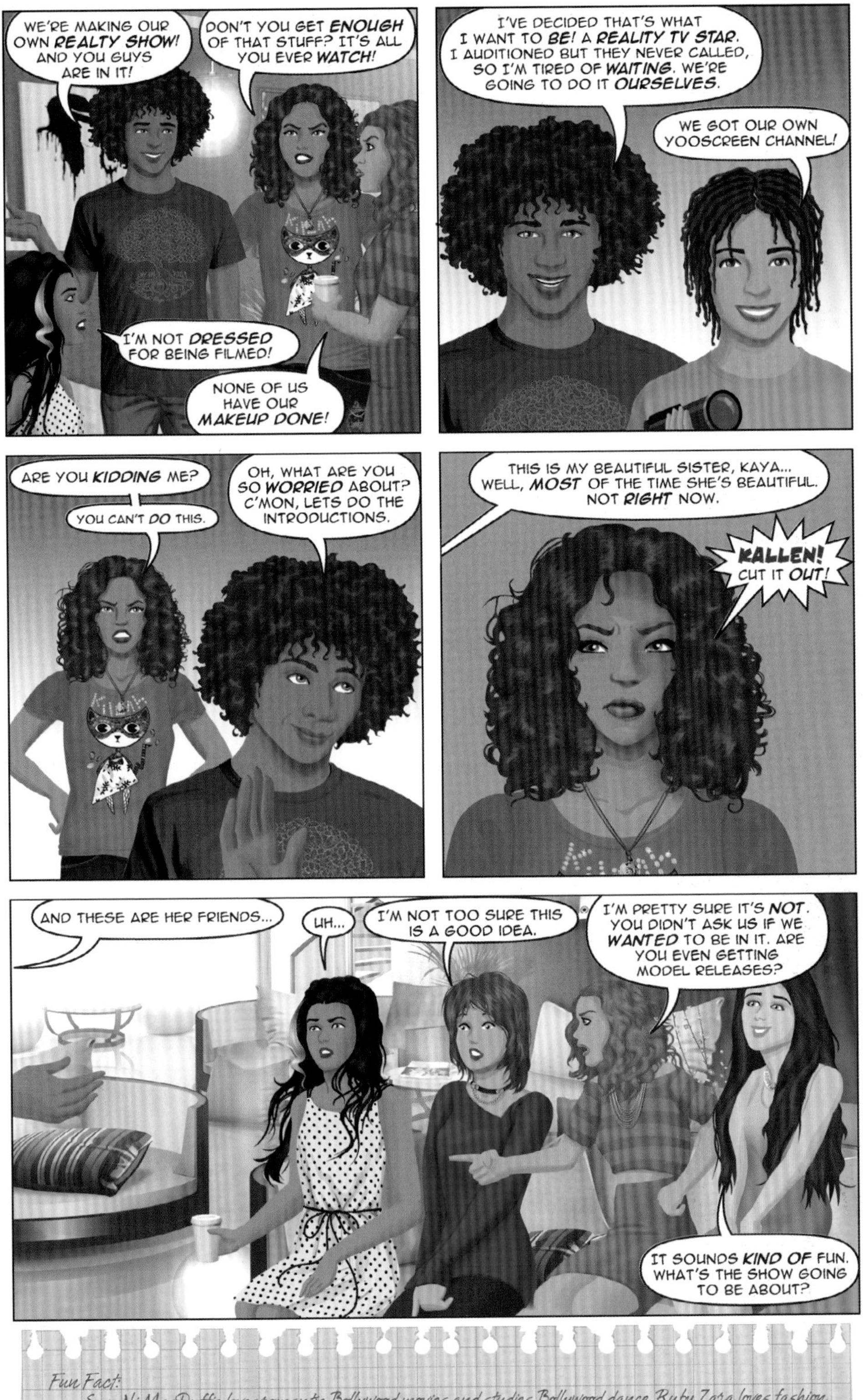
WE'RE MAKING OUR OWN REALTY SHOW! AND YOU GUYS ARE IN IT!
DON'T YOU GET ENOUGH OF THAT STUFF? IT'S ALL YOU EVER WATCH!
I'M NOT DRESSED FOR BEING FILMED!
NONE OF US HAVE OUR MAKEUP DONE!
I'VE DECIDED THAT'S WHAT I WANT TO BE! A REALITY TV STAR. I AUDITIONED BUT THEY NEVER CALLED, SO I'M TIRED OF WAITING. WE'RE GOING TO DO IT OURSELVES.
WE GOT OUR OWN YOOSCREEN CHANNEL!
ARE YOU KIDDING ME?
YOU CAN'T DO THIS.
OH, WHAT ARE YOU SO WORRIED ABOUT? C'MON, LETS DO THE INTRODUCTIONS.
THIS IS MY BEAUTIFUL SISTER, KAYA... WELL, MOST OF THE TIME SHE'S BEAUTIFUL. NOT RIGHT NOW.
KALLEN! CUT IT OUT!
AND THESE ARE HER FRIENDS...
UH...
I'M NOT TOO SURE THIS IS A GOOD IDEA.
I'M PRETTY SURE IT'S NOT. YOU DIDN'T ASK US IF WE WANTED TO BE IN IT. ARE YOU EVEN GETTING MODEL RELEASES?
IT SOUNDS KIND OF FUN. WHAT'S THE SHOW GOING TO BE ABOUT?

Fun Fact:
Sue-Ni MacDuffie loves romantic Bollywood movies and studies Bollywood dance. Ruby Zara loves fashion and technology and dreams of combining the two in unique ways.

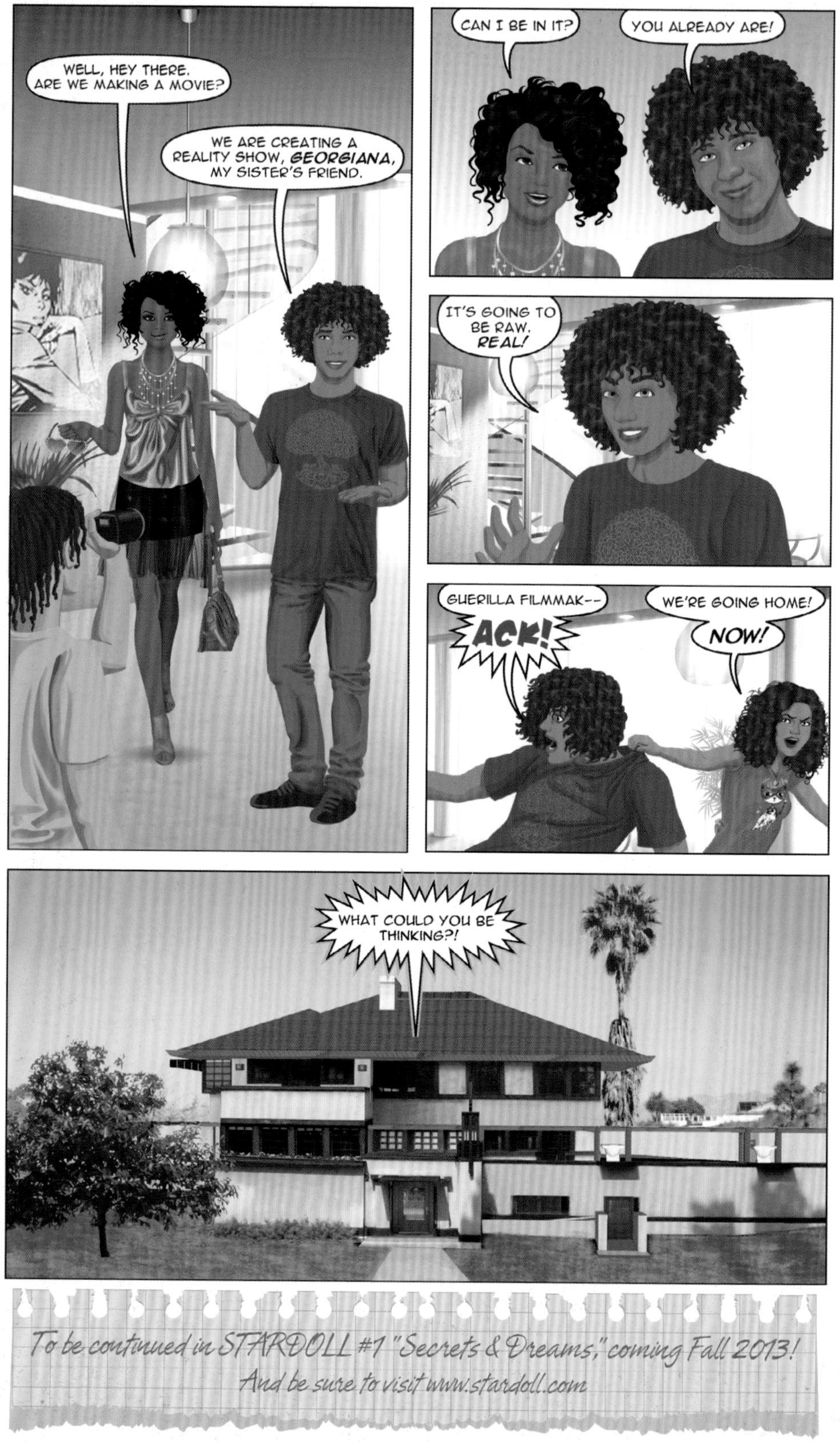
WELL, HEY THERE. ARE WE MAKING A MOVIE?
WE ARE CREATING A REALITY SHOW, GEORGIANA, MY SISTER'S FRIEND.
CAN I BE IN IT?
YOU ALREADY ARE!
IT'S GOING TO BE RAW. REAL!
GUERILLA FILMMAK--
ACK!
WE'RE GOING HOME!
NOW!
WHAT COULD YOU BE THINKING?!

To be continued in STARDOLL #1 "Secrets & Dreams," coming Fall 2013!
And be sure to visit www.stardoll.com

Don't Miss the First Graphic Novel—Coming Soon!

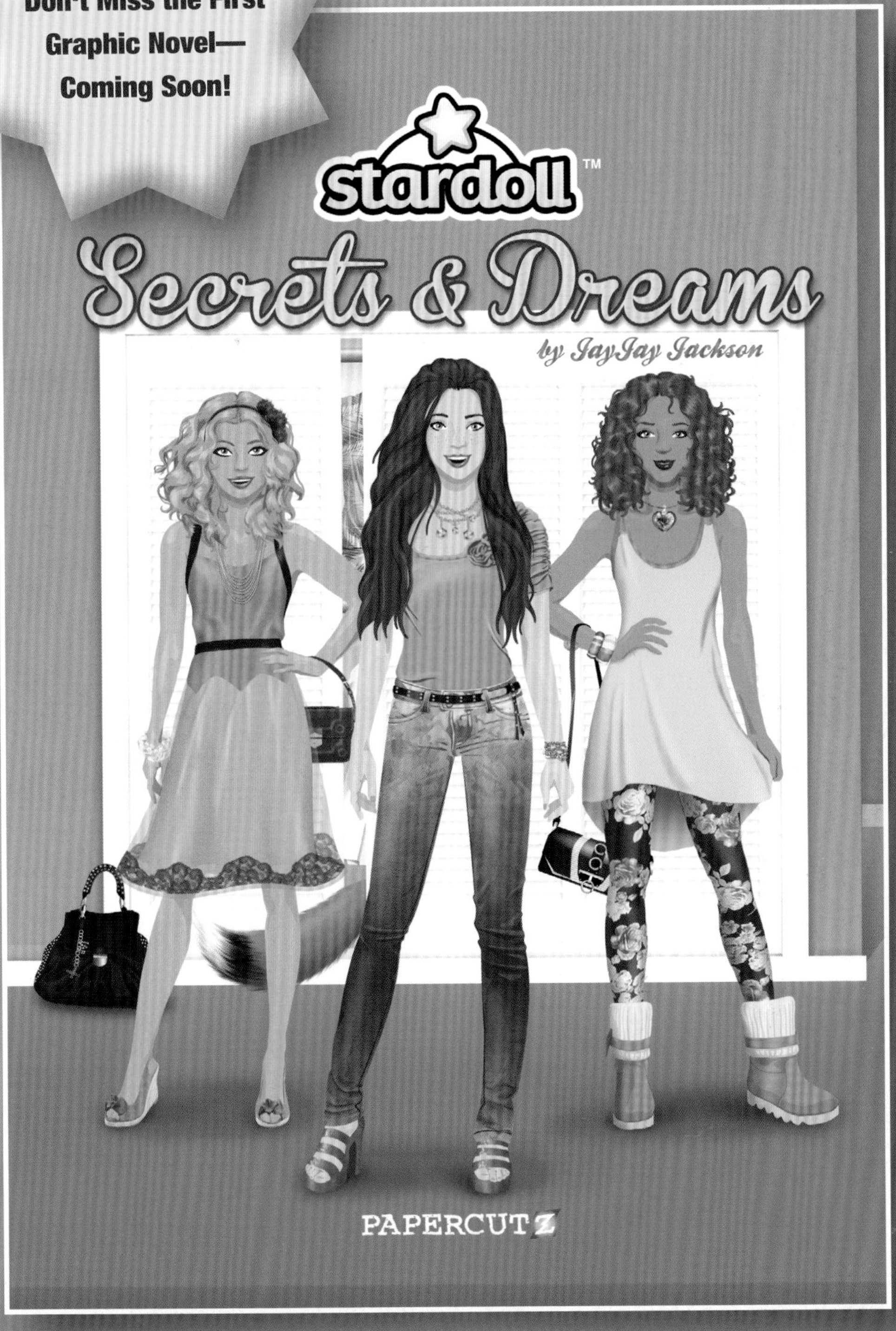
stardoll™
Secrets & Dreams
by JayJay Jackson
PAPERCUT Z

You've read her graphic novel...
Now read her diary!
Nancy Drew DIARIES™
Nancy Drew DIARIES™
Curse of the Arctic Star
CAROLYN KEENE
Nancy Drew DIARIES™
Strangers on a Train
CAROLYN KEENE
Nancy Drew DIARIES™
Mystery of the Midnight Rider
CAROLYN KEENE
Nancy Drew DIARIES™
Once Upon a Thriller
CAROLYN KEENE
Aladdin
SIMON & SCHUSTER Children's Publishing
Kids.SimonandSchuster.com
NancyDrew.com

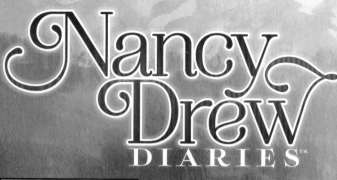

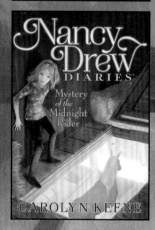

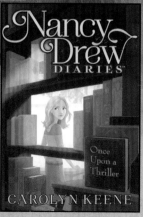

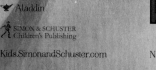